THE
BURDEN
OF
INNOCENCE

A NOVEL

JOHN
NARDIZZI

THE BURDEN OF INNOCENCE
© 2021, John F. Nardizzi

ISBN 978-1-7376876-0-3
eISBN 978-1-7376876-2-7

Please note that this is a crime novel and contains content that may disturb some readers, including scenes of violence, sexual assault/rape, and emotional/physical abuse.

"Hope is not a rock-solid thing... Hope erodes and it wears away until finally you wake up one day and you don't even realize that you don't have it anymore."

- BRIAN PEIXOTO

Dedicated to those who survive unjust imprisonment and live in grace. You are the real heroes.

- Dennis, Scott, Victor, Gary, James, Brian

PART 1
A SYSTEM OF JUSTICE

Boston, Massachusetts

CHAPTER 1

TWO BURLY GUARDS from the sheriff's department walked Sam Langford to the van. He noticed a newspaper wedged in a railing—his name jumped off the page in bold print: **Jury to Decide Langford's Fate In Waterfront Slaying.** The presumption of innocence was a joke. You took the guilt shower no matter what the jury decided. He thought of his mother then, and the old ladies like her, reading the headline as they sipped their morning coffee across the city. He was innocent. But they would hate him forever.

A guard shoved Langford's head below the roofline. He sat down in the cargo section, the only prisoner today. The guard secured him to a bar that ran the length of the floor, the chain rattling an icy tune. The van squealed off.

Langford's head felt so light it could drift right off his shoulders. The van lurched, and he slid on the cold metal bench. The driver bumped the van into some potholes. Langford dug his heels into the floor. This was a guard-approved amusement ride, bouncing felon maggots off good 'ol American steel. Sam had observed this man that morning. Something about his face was troubling. Sheriffs, guards, cops—most of them were okay. They didn't bother him because he didn't bother them. But cop work attracted certain men who hid their true selves; men with a vicious streak that could turn an average day into a private torture chamber. These men were cancers to be avoided. Average days were what he wanted in jail. No violent breaks in the tedium.

The van careened on and stopped at a loading dock of the hulking courthouse, which jutted in the sky like a pale granite finger accusing the heavens. The last day of trial. Outside, Langford saw TV news vans and raised satellite dishes, the reporters being primped and padded for the live shot. The rear doors opened and the guard's shaved skull appeared in silhouette. He tensed as the guard grabbed his arm and pulled him out. The guard wore a thin smile. "We'll take the smooth road back. Just for you," he muttered.

A clutch of photographers hovered behind a wall above the dock. Langford looked up at the blue sky, as he always did, focusing on breathing deeply. He would never assist, not for a minute, in his own degradation. He was innocent. He would not cooperate. Let them run their little circus, the cameras, the shouted questions, the boom microphones dropped over his head to pick up a stray utterance. He leveled his jaw and looked past them. He knew he had no chance with them.

The guards walked him inside the courthouse and to an elevator. The chains clanked as they swung with his movement. They took the elevator to the eighth floor where a court officer escorted the group into a hallway. Langford pulled his body erect toward the ceiling, as high as he could get. He intended to walk into the courtroom like some ancient Indian chieftain, unbowed. He was innocent and that sheer fact gave him some steel, yes it did.

The door opened and he stepped inside the courtroom. The gallery looked packed full, as usual. Cameras clicked. Low voices in the crowd hissed venom. "Death sentence is too good for you, asshole," whispered one. He whispered a bit too loudly. A court officer wasted no time, hustling over and guiding the man to the exit.

Langford walked ahead, keeping his dark eyes focused. His family might watch this someday. Some ragged old news clip showing their son's dark history. He struggled to keep the light burning behind his eyes. Something true, something eternal might show through. At least he hoped so. He had told his lawyer there would be no last-minute plea deal; he was innocent, and that was it.

As he walked, he felt the eyes of the crowd pick over him, watching for some involuntary tic that would betray his thoughts. But fear roiled in his belly. He was afraid, no doubt. He knew the old saying that convicted murderers sat at the head table in the twisted hierarchy of a prison. But the fact remained—every prisoner walked next to a specter of sudden violence. He desperately wanted to avoid prison.

Keys rattled in the high-ceilinged courtroom as the officers unchained him. He rubbed his wrists and then sat down at the defense table. His defense lawyer, George Sterling, took the seat next to him. He was dressed in a dark blue suit with a bright orange-yellow tie. The color seemed garish for the occasion.

"How you doing, Sam?"

"Hopeful. But ready for the worst."

Sterling grabbed his hand and shook it firmly. But his eyes betrayed him. Langford got the sense even his lawyer felt a catastrophe was coming.

The mother of the dead woman sat one row away from his own mother. Even here, mothers bore the greatest pain. Both women stared at him. Langford nodded to his mother as she mouthed the words, "I love you". He smiled briefly. He glanced at the mother of the dead girl but looked away. Her eyes blazed with hatred and pain. He wanted to say something, but the odds were impossible. The reporters would misconstrue any gesture; the court officers might claim he threatened her. He saw no way out. Even a basic act of human kindness became muddled in a courtroom.

A court officer yelled, "All rise." The whispers

died down, and the gallery rose. The judge came in from chambers in a black-robed flurry. The lawyers went to sidebar, that curious phenomenon where they gather and whisper at the judge's bench like kids in detention. Then the judge signaled the sidebar was over and told the court officer to bring in the jury. The jurors walked to the jury box, every one of them with a blank look fixed on their face. None of them met his eyes. One juror eventually looked over at him. He tried to gauge his fate in her flat eyes, the set of her face. But there was nothing to see.

As the judge and lawyers spoke, the lightheadedness left him. Everything came into focus. Langford watched the foreperson hand a slip of paper to a court officer. She took a few steps and handed the paper to the judge. The judge pushed gray hairs off her forehead, examined the paper, and placed it on her desk. A silence descended. Shuffles of feet, small muted coughs. People waited for a meteor to hit the earth. The clerk read the docket number into the record and the judge looked over to the foreperson, a woman with long dark hair and glasses. "On indictment 2001183 charging the defendant, Samuel Langford, with murder, what say you, Madame Foreperson? Is the defendant not guilty or guilty of murder in the first degree?"

"We find the defendant guilty of murder in the first degree."

To Langford, the words seemed unreal, from a world away. A mist slid over his eyes. Gasps of joy, cries of surprise. A few spectators began clapping. The judge banged the gavel. Someone sobbed behind him, and this sound he knew; his mother was crying openly now. His body petrified. He couldn't turn around.

Sterling put one hand on his shoulder, which snapped him back. The gesture irritated him. He didn't want to be touched. Sterling's junior assistant cupped his hand over his mouth. Sterling said something about the evidence. They would file an appeal. Langford stared at him. The reality of his new life began to emerge.

The process moved quickly, the ending like all good endings—neat, nothing overdone, but nothing left to wonder about, either. Court officers shackled him again and stood clasping his arms. The judge thanked the jury for their service. Langford felt overwhelmed by absurdity—they were being thanked for sending an innocent man to prison. The gulf between the truth and what was happening made him feel sick; they believed he had killed the poor woman. The judge told the lawyers to prepare for sentencing in a week. A guard pushed him through a door to the right and he could hear muffled sounds, people calling his name, as if the voices came through a dense fog over a distance. His head, floating, floating beyond the real.

It was over.

Down the long corridor they moved him, toward the rear lot and the prisoner's dock. A flock of reporters circled the van. "Any comment, Mr. Langford?" "Mr. Langford, will you appeal this verdict?" "Do you want to say something to the family of the victim?" Then a hand pushed down on the back of his head and he stooped inside the van. The guard chained him to the floor. There was that slight smile on his lips.

The engine shot to life. Langford waited for the door to close. Sludge ran through his veins. He closed his eyes and let despair surge through his heart.

CHAPTER 2

15 years later

IN A CORNER at the Sanchez Boxing Gym in the South End, Ray Infantino braced his lean frame, fired a jab, threw a left hook off the jab, and smashed an overhand right. The heavy bag jerked on the chain like a drunken tourist caught out late in the wrong part of town. He moved around the heavy bag, feet sliding, not hopping. He threw another right cross and then switched stances, the right foot in the lead. He hooked a low right followed by an overhead left. His father showed him that move when he was a kid. He stopped once the bell rang for the end of the round. Sweat poured off his toned physique.

He pulled off the gloves to tighten his hand wraps. He wrapped his hands the way his father had taught him: loop the thumb and then through the fingers, making the fist a steel ball. It pissed him off when he saw other fighters not wrapping between the fingers, a lack of finesse he found appalling.

There was action all over the gym—sparring in the three rings, prospects putting in their bag work, trainers barking out instructions. Two young men gathered nearby and watched him. They were new. Ray had never seen them before. After he finished his workout, one of them ventured toward him.

"You fight pretty good."

"Thanks."

"Hope I'm good as you when I'm that old."

Ray whipped a fist toward the guy and stopped an inch from his face. The guy's mouth gaped. His friend broke out laughing. Ray walked away and pointed at the man. "Show some respect when you come in here," he said. "Forty ain't old."

He laughed and headed to the showers. The last few days had been a rare respite from the grind. When his case involving a missing woman in the San Francisco underworld hit the news, his business boomed. He was a name now. That was how it worked in the legal business. When you were newsworthy, clients deemed it safe to pay large retainers up front, and he could decline work he didn't want. He still kept his black hair long in back and kept lean and fit, preserving the illusion of youth, but he knew his time in this business was closer to the end than the beginning. By the end of the case in San Francisco, he had come to accept what happened. His old life was gone forever. His relationship with Dominique did not seem like it would survive. But the haunted rims below his eyes faded and he felt reinvigorated, ready for new challenges.

He headed out for a coffee at a cafe across the street. Last year, his doctor advised him he should cut down, but he felt it was a minor vice. Not healthy to deny the small things that made life worth living. He took a seat in the window. He appreciated his new place in the South End. Long a home to Latino and Black families, the 1990s brought an influx of new residents like him to the old brownstones—downtown office workers, architects, gay couples—looking for the rich canvas of city living. Block by block, cafes and restaurants were renovated, old wood paneling stripped and refurbished, the construction boom rolling out toward Massachusetts Avenue. He enjoyed walking the uneven brick sidewalks and coming upon vestiges of the old neighborhood: a bookstore packed with two floors of hardcovers in an old brownstone, the painted letters on a brick wall of the long-closed Sahara restaurant, hollyhocks that bloomed from a tucked-away corner.

His cell phone rang and he saw the call forwarded from his office. He remembered that his receptionist Sheri had taken the day off.

"Ray Infantino Agency, how can I help you?"

"Hi, this is Dan Stone. I'm a defense lawyer here in Boston. I got your name from a lawyer I met at a bar event—you came highly recommended. Wondering if you might be able to help me on an old murder case. I'm going to see a new client, Sam Langford. Not sure if you heard about the case, it began over fifteen years ago."

"I don't remember it."

"Langford's case was high profile at the time. A violent rape-murder on the waterfront. The trial brought out the worst: witnesses with serious drug addictions, rogue cops. People thought Langford looked like the cleanest guy in the courthouse. But the jury still convicted. There was a dead girl. Someone needed to pay. Langford was easy. Not necessarily the right guy, but he was the available target."

Ray was used to this nonsense from defense lawyers. No one was guilty in their world. Still, he recalled now that he had heard something of Stone: bright guy, a plugger in the courtroom, well prepared rather than depending on flashy trial antics.

"I'm going to see him this week and wanted to reach out to see if you would come with me. Schedule permitting. We have learned a few things, and he says he wants to talk over the next steps. I believe he is innocent, Ray. He's been trying for close to fifteen years to prove it. You know the standard in these cases. Very high bar."

"Cops are allowed a lot of leeway to be wrong."

"Right. We have to show intent, or at least recklessness, when it comes to police misconduct. If we can uncover new evidence, I would plan on filing a motion for a new trial within a year." Stone went blabbing on about the legal issues. "So what do you think?"

He had time to take it on. "Is this a private case?"

Stone hesitated. "No. I'm appointed by the public defender's office."

"Impossible odds and crappy pay. How can I resist?"

Stone laughed. "Okay then. I know this is real short notice, but any chance you're free this afternoon?"

Ray checked his schedule. "That's fine. Where's he held?"

"Walpole. There was an incident at the max so they moved him there."

"I'll meet you in the lobby at 1:00 p.m."

Ray hung up the phone and stood up, gazing out the window at the copper rooftops. The odds were terrible in such cases. He thought back to his father Leo and how they had destroyed him. He decided that the next time there was an uneven fight, he would ensure the little guy had a weapon.

* * *

Ray showered and combed his dark hair back before dressing in a pinstriped blue suit with a pale yellow shirt and a patterned tie. Prison guards treated you well if you dressed in a suit; they thought you were a defense lawyer or a bureaucrat in charge of the prison budget.

He walked to the garage behind the office. He drove a Jeep most of the time. But he was in the midst of a love affair with his latest rig, a 1965 Shelby Cobra convertible that he traded as payment from a client and drove during the summer. Metallic silver paint, white bucket seats. In a cruel world, sitting in those seats made him feel clean and holy, at least for a while.

The summer heat rippled off the highway as he drove down to Walpole State Prison, officially renamed Cedar Junction on account of sensitive citizens who resented their bucolic town being associated with a prison. No one used the name Cedar Junction, and the place was still just called Walpole by anyone not working for the government. The name change would never obscure the essence of the place, a mournful gray bruise in the woods, as if the accumulated misery of the men inside was leaching the color from the trees. At night, enormous floodlights contended with the mist creeping from the woods, giving the walls a sepulchral appearance.

Ray parked near the administrative building outside the walls and walked into the stark lobby, where all visitors were processed. He filled out the intake sheet and checked the box for a client visit. Then he placed his keys and wallet into a metal locker, removed the orange-handled key, and moved to the body scanner. He kept on his black brogue shoes but removed his leather belt.

A guard, young, cheerful, waved him through. "You've been here before."

"Few times."

He passed through the machine. A steel door slid open and Ray stepped into a long corridor. The guard walked him outside to the cell block. They crossed the yard and entered another lobby. Ray saw a few cramped interview rooms painted yellow and bereft of any human markers. The air smelled of disinfectant. A man in a suit sat in the room furthest to the left, slouched back in a plastic chair. A stack of legal documents lay in front of him. Ray walked inside.

"Ray?" the man asked, looking up. "Good to see you. I'm Dan Stone." Ray reached out and Stone grabbed his hand in a steel grip as if trying to prove his manhood in a place filled with brutal men.

The guard retreated and sat in a chair in the middle of the lobby, watching the rooms with half-hearted interest. In the distance, Ray could hear the clanging of metal doors closing. He looked up at the white ceiling.

"I always assume that they bug these rooms," Ray muttered.

Stone laughed. "You're more paranoid than I am." He nodded toward the guard. "They sit out there and try to listen to everything we say."

A rapping on the glass window, and Ray looked up to see the guard marching a prisoner across the concrete floor. He had his first look at Sam Langford. Appearing to be in his fifties, his pale face set off by dark hair flecked with silver, Langford had maintained a lean build that looked resistant to the high-starch diet that prisons seemed to force on inmates. Bright orange overalls and sneakers of unknown make, no laces. He kept a flat stare in his eyes that seemed to take him beyond the walls. Man may be a creature who can adjust to anything, but Ray saw a resistance in Langford, a refusal to accept his circumstances, that he liked immediately. Langford reached out to shake Ray's hand and then Stone's.

Langford sat down at the table. It felt stifling inside the room now, with three men jammed inside, knees bumping under the table. Ray caught the smell of soap again, industrial-strength prison stuff, this time coming from Langford's clothing. They talked a bit about the prison and the restrictions on books— the guards seized most crime novels, and anything like Harry Potter. "It's kind of a random policy," Langford said. "I'm dying for something new."

"I was just telling Ray about your case," said Stone. "Why don't you fill us in, Sam?"

Langford nodded. "Well, let me start from the beginning. I'm from Dorchester. I moved away to work in the Vegas construction boom in the eighties. Hundred-foot hole-in-the-wall condos in the middle of the desert selling for three hundred grand. Anyway, I came back home—my mom's still in Savin Hill. So I go see her, right? There's this neighborhood guy, Davin Price, who I knew since we were kids. He's still around. He's never left, never had anything to leave for."

Ray watched Sam recount the story in a direct but soft voice.

"I hear things when I get back, Davin's now working as an informant. I never run into this guy. Never see him or have any dealings. So one day I'm at the pub, The Nines on Dot Ave. A cop comes in and someone jokes, 'There goes the bad lieutenant.' You know, after the movie?"

"Harvey Keitel."

"Yeah, Keitel. Great film. So this guy says the old cop is rotten. Faviola, I think his name was. Money problems, got divorced, went off the deep end. And this guy says Price was Faviola's street connect. There was a second guy involved, too, Faviola's partner, Scott Magnus."

Langford was in a groove now. "That was where it got interesting. Up to this point, I never saw Faviola in my life. Wouldn't know him from jack squat. We hear later on, it's in the papers, this girl is found dead on the waterfront. Near the electric plant. Tough place at night. Doesn't make sense she would be there. Well, Davin Price and this other guy, Joey Butters, are talking to people. Butters is telling people that I was there at the bar that night. They wanna know if anyone knows anything they can pass on. It's fucking bullshit!"

Stone jumped in. "At trial they produce these two witnesses, Butters and Price. Butters especially fucking kills us. He puts Sam there at the bar, says he saw him come out of the bar that night with the victim, Katie Donnegan."

"The Electric House Pub, a Southie hangout," said Langford.

"Right. Butters is a waste product, with drug convictions and a reputation as the town drunk. This cop we mentioned, Magnus, investigates the murder and finds a stripper who confirms Butters' story. They line these three clowns up and his trial lawyer can't put a dent in them. A fucking sideshow."

"Where were you that night?" Ray asked, looking at Langford.

"I was walking home late. I live right by there. But I never went in that bar that night. I never seen that poor girl Katie."

"Been in the bar before?"

"Oh sure, Electric House is the neighborhood joint."

"So someone would have known you could be set up there." Ray said. He glanced over at Stone. "What do you need me to do?"

"For starters, we need to locate Butters and Price. Do more work on them, find out how deep they went as informants. Then interview them, especially Butters. He's the key." Stone paused. "This could be a particularly nasty bit of work, especially given the reputation of some of the cops involved. Faviola's dead now, but the others who are still around, well, they're gonna be tough. I asked around. Rumor has it that Magnus is connected. No one seems to want to talk about him. My usual police contacts—no one was willing to say a thing. There's a genuine fear when it comes to him."

Ray was drawn to these cases because they were the ultimate challenge in the investigative business. The impact of a dirty cop could be deadly. If you hired a bad plumber, the faucet leaked. If you had a corrupt cop investigating a murder, the guilty man remained untouched while an innocent man slept beneath a light bulb in a concrete box.

Cases like this reminded him of his father. He didn't hesitate.

"I'm in," said Ray.

Sam let a small sliver of a smile cross his face.

"One other thing. I didn't want to get into it on the phone, but I heard yesterday that Sam's brother will pay your fees. He owns a software firm in Waltham. If it was doing as well then as it is now, maybe Sam wouldn't be here."

"What do you mean?"

"His lawyer never hired an investigator. He did nothing in terms of investigation before the trial."

"Unreal."

Stone frowned. "Lawyer was disbarred a year after the trial. He was an alcoholic. But the cases he worked in prior years, that legal work stands. No appeal based on the mere fact he was found to be an incompetent drunk."

Ray shook his head in disgust. "Sam, you got both ends of it."

Sam leaned forward toward Ray, looking him long in the eyes. "I'm innocent, Ray. I don't want to die here."

Ray stared at him but said nothing. He resisted the lure to promise a garden when the way ahead was a hedge of thorns. But he felt something for this earnest man sitting next to him in prison scrubs. The old lure was there, the blood rush that came with discovering buried evidence, nothing like it in the world.

They stood in the small room, a legal fellowship formed amid the gray concrete. Sam and Ray shook hands.

"Thank you for taking it on."

"Don't thank me yet," Ray said with a frown. "I'll do a lot more than poke around. But we have a long way to go."

CHAPTER 3

AFTER SAM LEFT, Ray and Stone walked down a gray corridor back to the security desk. A female guard asked them to show their hand stamps. Stone placed the back of his hand under the ultraviolet light. Ray realized he had no stamp—the prison guard had forgotten to stamp him before the visit.

"Sorry, I don't have one."

The guard looked at him. "You don't have a hand stamp. That's a problem." They stared at each other. The guard reached for a phone and spoke to someone to verify Ray had just been inside the visiting room. Then the guard hung up.

"You don't have a hand stamp," the guard said again.

"Didn't know that was my job." Ray shot back.

The guard pondered this in silence. Then the gate opened. Stone grinned as he and Ray walked out of the doorway to the prison parking lot.

"So what do you think, Ray?"

"I like him. Straight shooter. Tough case, though. So many years back."

"Yes." Stone took off his coat and tossed it in back of his car. Ray could see sweat stains under his shirt.

"Hot in there, Dan?"

"I feel this heat now. I must be getting old." He sighed. They stood by the car while Stone picked through his trunk and handed Ray a copy of the file, a full box of documents. They talked about the next steps and then said their farewells.

Ray drove away through the leafy cover of the back roads near the prison. He thought about the older cases he had worked on that involved rogue cops and the blue line of testilying. He hated dirty cops with a special passion. Because police responded first to a crime scene, their actions took place in secret, away from the public eye. They interviewed witnesses and secured fingerprint or DNA evidence that could solve a case. Over the years, Ray had investigated cops who went off the rails and over the edge—abusing witnesses, threatening to arrest people if they didn't tell a story the way the cop wanted, ignoring evidence that didn't fit their theory or tossing it away into cold harbor waters. He had seen all these things happen as innocent men were framed and time dissolved each passing day behind prison walls.

He headed back to his office in the South End and pulled the Mustang into the garage. The streets were bustling with activity: kids in headphone cocoons, babysitters speaking lilting Spanish to a line of five kids holding a rope to stop them from rushing into traffic. Inside, the office was quiet. He placed the Langford case file on his desk and took a breath. The desk was modern, some kind of black metal. He wasn't sure he liked it yet. The old desk had some history, but it didn't fit here. Maybe someday he would be retired in similar fashion: still working but out of time.

But he had discovered that old things could pack a nasty wallop.

He spent the next four hours reading through the old case file and beginning a task memo. Drug-addled witnesses, destined for the bottom, permeated the case. Especially Joseph C. Butters, called Joey by everyone. At trial, Butters had claimed that he was walking on Summer Street around the time of the murder. Two women got into a taxi but then got back out. Beneath the streetlights, he noticed people on the sidewalk outside of the bar, a man arguing with a woman. He had pointed dramatically at Langford at the trial—"Him. Right there, that's the man I saw."

Ray examined the documents provided to the defense team at trial. Butters and Price were both career snitches who had testified in several trials. There were copies of checks written out to Butters and Price for odd amounts, drawn on state accounts. One check was written out for $234.34. What the hell did a snitch do to earn that exact amount of money? He read through the reports of his handlers. In one case, they inserted Butters into the same cell as a murder suspect; he testified in that trial, which resulted in a conviction. Later, he got his own case pled down to a misdemeanor and time served. Information on just how many cases Butters had testified in was missing. Only rarely had Ray seen a careful accounting of that aspect; these guys were akin to federal employees, but no one could tell how long they worked. One report from 1995 showed that Butters' flow of information seemed to slow. He had not worked on any cases for several years.

Both Butters and Price claimed they received nothing from the prosecutor for their testimony on the Langford case—on this one, they were just unpaid eyewitnesses. Just doing the legal system a good turn. But how did that fit with the drop-off in paid informant work for Butters? What did they promise these two men? It all looked suspicious.

He wasn't sure yet if Sam was innocent, but the case was what he wanted. He knew a case like this would push him. There were reasons he did investigations, personal reasons like what happened with his father. And if he was honest with himself, there was another reason, simpler, something that crossed over to pride: He felt good when hunting people down. In his experience, people liked to express their talents. When he picked out subtleties in the data and the investigation came together, he felt something uncurl in his belly and send shivers up his spine. It was the best feeling he ever felt.

Ray ran database searches to locate other key witnesses. A friend of the victim who had been with her at the bar that night died in a car accident a few years later. Several police officers who investigated the case were dead. Ray ran through the media coverage of the case and saw an article where a reporter had dug into Butters' past. The reporter tried to meet with a man named Gerry DeCosta at Butters' old apartment. DeCosta offered "no comment" and not a speck more. The article described DeCosta as a "former roommate who was arrested once for assaulting Butters." Ray smiled—that was a relationship he could exploit. There was a good reason why a scumbag like Butters got punched in the face.

The assault took place in the same year as the Langford trial.

Ray ran some more database searches and found that DeCosta lived near the harbor in Gloucester. He would go see DeCosta right away. It always started like this, a simple conversation with a ghost from the past.

He went out to the garage and took the Shelby out for a cruise, bumping his way north on the pockmarked highway toward Cape Ann and the old fishing port of Gloucester.

On the waterfront, he could smell the salt air tang as he drove past the Fisherman's Memorial, the statue of a captain straining at the wheel of his craft. A plaque read: "They that go down to the sea in ships..." The rough and tumble harbor seemed a fitting spot for those who fished and died in dark waters.

DeCosta lived on a spit of land across from a row of rusty canneries. The August heat trapped the smell of decaying fish along the waterfront. Ray stopped at DeCosta's walkup apartment, a little hovel with peeling paint and a sofa rotting on the front lawn. The sofa's springs were erupting through the fabric at all angles, a parody of comfort and welcome. Ray shook his head and went to ring the front doorbell but saw only broken wires jutting from a hole. He rapped on the door with his knuckles.

A voice from behind the door said, "Who is it?"

"Hi, I'm trying to reach Gerry DeCosta."

"Who is it?"

"Gerry, this is Ray Infantino, I'm looking into a criminal case involving an old friend of yours—Mr. Butters—"

"He's no friend of mine."

"That's why I said old. Can we talk for a minute?"

He heard the bolt slide back and an intense, wiry, dark-haired man stepped away from the open door. He wore no shirt and looked like Iggy Pop, minus the drug recovery interventions. "So you're not working for Butters?" DeCosta said.

"I work for a guy he set up."

DeCosta smiled. "That sounds like Butters. What a piece of shit. His momma probably wishes she took birth control instead of getting a son like that."

Ray nodded at the sentiment. "I wouldn't bet on it. Mothers forgive everything."

DeCosta invited him in and they walked down

a dim hallway. DeCosta moved with a strange, piston-like gait as if heavy weights were dragging each hand. He sat down in the kitchen, a nasty slice of bachelorhood boasting stained Formica counters and a fetid odor of endless nights of cheap takeout. A knife crusted with food particles rested on the table. Ray noticed a stove with no door.

"Cook much?" he said.

"Takeout, bro. There's a good Chinese place around the corner. General Gau's chicken."

"The unknown general."

DeCosta guffawed. "Yeah, weird they name takeout chicken after the military. So what did that prick Butters do to your guy?"

"He testified against him. Testified falsely, we believe."

"How did you find me?"

"There was a news article that mentioned you roomed with him. Something about a minor altercation." He paused as DeCosta's face darkened and let him pick up the thread.

"Yeah, we were living at this place for a few years. He was my tenant, actually. I put an ad in the paper looking for a roommate and got fucking Butters. What luck, huh? The tenant from hell! The guy tried to sell all my fuckin' clothes while I was in jail!" He sat back and looked out the window.

"What happened?"

DeCosta threw his head back and laughed. "Well, I tried to kill him. He drove me to it!"

"I hear he has that effect."

"The cops got me for brandishing a weapon on him. At first, Butters was not a problem. He acted nice. Everything was going alright. Then Butters started telling me about how he was a big shot, how he worked undercover for the feds. I didn't believe him. Told me he got paid by the FBI. Sure buddy, we all work for the feds, right?"

"What did he say he was doing for them?"

"Gave them information on things."

"Anything specific?"

"Well, he was working on a murder case, that was how he put it. 'Working a murder.' As if Butters ever held a job."

"What did he say about it?"

"A guy murdered this girl in Boston. Some bar near the harbor."

"Any names?"

"Nah. He kept it vague."

"So how did it break down between you and him?"

"He was just driving me crazy, man. Dropped the nice boy stuff and turned into Mr. Hyde. I was missing things. It was him. I couldn't prove it was him so I tried to scare him once and, you know, took out my gun. He had called the cops and when they came, the timing was real bad. I had my gun out. Properly licensed, I will add. I chased him around the house!" DeCosta laughed.

"You can't do that in this era," Ray said.

"Yeah, I know. It's too bad. So much for the Second Amendment. Damn thing is dead."

Ray stretched in his chair. "So he got under your skin a bit."

"You can definitely say that."

"What else did he say about the murder case?"

"He gave no names. Just said he saw some guy somewhere on the waterfront that night. And that he was the key witness for the trial. It always cracked me up to think someone would rely on Butters for anything. Key witness, what bullshit."

"What else did he say about seeing that guy?"

"I think he was driving a cab then."

"Really?"

"Yeah. Not sure it was a legit cab, though. More like a gypsy cab. He picked up guys at the airport, did odd jobs for guys in South Boston."

They talked for a while longer, but DeCosta had little to add. Ray thanked him; the information about the taxi would be useful. DeCosta trotted over to the fridge for a can of Narragansett. They stepped outside. The heat had lifted and a salty mist blew into the cove.

"I hope it works out for your guy," DeCosta said. "Butters, he's a leech. He infects his environment. I hope you cook him."

CHAPTER 4

BACK AT THE office, Ray went through the trial testimony again and studied how Butters and Price
were used to build a case against Langford. Trials
were often built on such characters. While the court
system relied on an ancient facade of power—marble
columns that recalled Greek and Roman temples,
black-robed judges with solemn voices recalling the
devotion of monks—the fact was that cases orbited
around more shabby and tawdry things. Damaged
characters like DeCosta and Butters took on starring
roles, mouthing their lines and then disappear-
ing offscreen, never to be seen again. Drug addicts
testified about events they barely recalled, or they
cooked up a story on the spot. Most jurors were
hardworking, earnest—retired folks, students, flex-
ible workers—but a jury of peers could include a
sprinkling of racists and idiots. And while untrained
in reading body language, jurors were expected to
stare down practiced liars like Butters and Price to

render a verdict. So while the entire system was built on a belief in the granite rule of law, anyone close to it knew the pilings rested on quicksand, the whole damned legal shithouse sliding toward the abyss.

Ray read through the case file late into the night. It was time to look deeper into shadows from the past.

* * *

The next morning he woke late to sun streaming in the window. He felt refreshed. He grabbed a banana and devoured it on the way to the gym to pound out some time on the rowing machine. After a quick shower at the house, he put on a blue linen coat, jeans, and a pair of tan loafers. He thought of calling Dominique, but he didn't really want to talk. After their reunion in San Francisco, the past year or two had been all downhill. They hadn't broken up, exactly, but the warm feelings faded to cold dust. He felt responsible for most of that, but didn't know how to fix it.

He called Neil Robinson, the retired Boston Police detective who had investigated the Langford case. Ray had noticed Robinson's name in the case file and figured he would talk: Robinson was working as a defense investigator now. Robinson was willing to meet, and suggested a cafe near Lewis Wharf in the North End, the cramped old Italian neighborhood of Boston where snippets of the mother tongue still rang out in certain cafes. It was once the headquarters of the Boston branch of La Cosa Nostra, but the group had seen its power dwindle over the years. The neighborhood was always bigger than brazen goodfellas. Real estate prices soared and dozens of restaurants and cafes did a booming business among the brick alleys, from modern bistros with shiny furnishings to old-style places with ornate woodwork that looked like private social clubs.

As Ray walked into the cafe, he caught the delectable scent of fresh Scala bread, garlic, and grilled meat. The cafe owner completed his assault on the senses by hiring young women with visa problems to work as servers. Ray took a seat at a table. The sun shone down from the ceiling-to-floor windows. As Ray looked around, he figured out why Robinson had picked the place. Men flocked to the joint to let the atmosphere pull them away to the old country, where they had enjoyed some never-forgotten fling with a girl whose name faded with time but whose face shimmered in memory and left them with a beautiful feeling of utter loss.

At just before 11:00 a.m., a compact man of medium height stepped inside, looked around, and then locked eyes on Ray. Robinson wore glasses but looked much younger than his sixty years; more librarian than cop. He sported a dapper look with a blazer, pocket handkerchief, and cap. They shook hands and ricocheted some names off each other, people they knew in the detective business.

"So you're looking into the Langford case," he said. "It's about time. You got tough sledding ahead."

The young waitress came, and they ordered coffee. "Wish I spoke Italian," muttered Robinson.

"There's an old saying: Speak Spanish to God, French to the king, and Italian to women. And German to your dog."

Robinson laughed. "What about speaking Portuguese—she's probably Brazilian."

"True." Ray said. "So when did you start on the force?"

"Started in Roxbury in late 1980s. Welcome to the jungle. Christ, there was more action in Roxbury in a day than there was in the rest of the city all year. I was in the gang unit. My commanding officer was the start of my disillusionment. That piece of shit, Magnus."

Ray was surprised that Robinson spoke so candidly. Ex-cops could be tricky interviews. They liked to spar, a verbal jousting session. Other times, the blue wall of silence rose and the guy wouldn't say a thing. But Robinson was a different character, Ray could sense it. Robinson had the balls of an independent operator.

Ray decided he would get right to the point. "So then you went to the dark side. Defense work."

Robinson smiled. "It wasn't hard. I saw things," he said. "After spending twenty years putting people in jail, I see the value of the other side."

"A few lawyers who know you, including Dan Stone, told me they thought you were a standup guy. Someone who's interested in competence, not just the fact that the other guy wears a blue uniform."

"I know Stone. He's an excellent lawyer. What are you looking at now?"

"Based on the files I have seen, two career informants, Joey Butters and Davin Price, were portrayed as actual witnesses who just stumbled onto the crime scene at the right time. But I don't buy it."

"I never did either. Price, I used him. He was a long-term guy, connected." Robinson's nostrils flared. "But I hated the prick. Arrogant. Talked a great game, but his deliveries were shit—low-level guys, mafia soldiers. Never the top guys."

"So why was he kept on?"

"We had orders to use him. Someone liked him upstairs."

"Who?"

"Magnus, that was his boy. He loved the guy, they grew up together."

"Friends in low places," said Ray. He knew it might come to this, a command officer protecting a sociopath just because they grew up in the same housing project.

Robinson continued. "Magnus said the guy had connections into LCN in Providence, the Patriarca crime family. Like I said, there was little to show for it. We only built bullshit gambling cases with him, that kind of thing. I mean, come on. We had a couple busts on the North Shore, informal card games at the VFW, plastic tables, a few grand in the kitty. Old men whining about their prostates over some cheap wine. Never any big names. This guy did not impress me."

"What's your impression of Magnus?"

For the first time, a shadow crossed Robinson's face. "There is something to be worried about with him. Nasty guy. Watch your back. Knew him in high school. Even then, he was a bully. But he changed. Or covered it up just enough to slip through the academy."

"How much did he do on Langford's case?"

"That I was never sure of. He was my commanding officer then. He got known for rock 'n rolling the perps. A guy resisted arrest, he'd bump their squash off the door as he put them in the cruiser. Kick in the ribs, the whole bit. Just a sadistic fucking guy. There were at least three or four IA investigations into the guy but nothing amounted to anything. One time he held open one eye of a female perp and blasted her with pepper spray."

"Did you see him do that?"

"No, but it sounds right. Sick little twist on everything."

"Why did you get pulled off the case?"

"I learned they rounded up Joey Butters as a witness in Langford's case. That's like building a case around the town drunk. I spoke to Magnus and told him I'd interview him myself. Next thing, Magnus reassigned me to some other case. I was young. I had no pull, so there was nothing I could do."

Ray sipped his coffee. "What do you know about Magnus' informant network?"

"Women usually, drug addicts, prostitutes. There were rumors he set them up on arrests and then let them work off the charges at sex parties with some cops. Expected them to perform." Robinson shook his head in disgust.

"Any names?"

"No. They keep all that information at headquarters. And they don't like me much over there."

A few kids came in and sat in silence at a table, texting on their phones. Robinson looked over and shook his head. "These kids don't even know how to talk to a live person anymore."

They sat for a minute while Ray reviewed his notes.

"So, what was your theory of this murder at the time?"

"I always wanted a hard look at a guy named McBain. Interviewed him at the time. Tough guy. Ran his crew out of the bar where the girl was killed. He had a history of this kind of shit with women. A rape charge, dismissed when the victim didn't show. Several assaults."

"Anyone follow up?"

"Doubt it. Once Butters made his ID, all lines led to your guy Langford. Everyone seemed to overlook McBain." He frowned.

"I need to talk to Butters," said Ray. "I have him living in the North End. Sound right?"

"Yeah, I remember we once picked him up somewhere down off Hanover and Fleet." Robinson took a sip of coffee. "I seem to recall Butters had a girlfriend in Roxbury. Black girl, real pretty."

"Always love talking with the ex-girlfriend. Tongue will go into fifth gear."

"Yeah, she's worth a visit. I used to meet him at her place off Columbus. Here, let me look for her name." He looked at his phone. "Maleah Scott." He showed Ray her old address, and Ray punched it into his phone. "I hate what Magnus does, I really do," said Robinson. "And Butters might be a way in, he might talk to you. He's a waste product. You can work him. He's easily intimidated. I'm thinking by now his years of zero production might catch up to him. Now the other guy, Price, I'd forget about him. He's more savvy."

"What did they have on Butters to get him to snitch?"

"B&Es, arson. He's been fucking up since 9th grade. Everyone we knew went to the trades or to work for the state. Or joined the military. But Butters just lingered and graduated into smack. Any powder he could snort or inject. He started robbing houses to cover his habit. Then there was an arson case involving an old mill in Roxbury. A young kid died in that fire, a runaway or something. Butters was facing manslaughter and started cooperating. Low-level stuff. Stick him in a cell and chat them up. He thought he was smooth, he'd tell us he was going to butter them up," laughed Robinson.

"Ever use him?"

"Once or twice, but I didn't trust him. Too unstable. The king of smalltime grift. He never produced.

I was doing gang investigations, and the brothers would never talk to a guy like him."

The waitress came back. Robinson gazed at her like he wanted to squeeze himself a juicy glass of Argentinian waitress. But he held his tongue and just smiled.

Ray made a motion with his notebook that he was done and ready to roll.

"Follow up with me anytime you need," said Robinson. "I'm glad to see someone is still working this case. It means something."

CHAPTER 5

RAY TOOK THE subway back to his place and ran Butters' girlfriend through his locator databases. New addresses came up, scattered around the same neighborhood. He walked to the garage. He dropped the top on the Shelby and headed to Jamaica Plain, the flatlands near the Charles River. People were flocking to the streets to enjoy the sun. It was early in the afternoon, no traffic; it would be a pleasant ride. A long time ago, JP had been a blue-collar neighborhood sprinkled with Latinos as you headed toward Mission Hill. But the ensuing years had seen young couples who worked downtown buying up the large old homes, paying a premium over asking prices and dabbing wild greens and purples on the old Victorians. Now it was unaffordable to most people.

Ray looked around and shook his head, recalling the days when he walked the streets as a young buck, getting ice cream at Marlowe's Corner Store, with its endless rows of candy boxes. You filled a brown bag with caramels, jelly beans, and Bottle Caps for a few nickels and sucked the sugar all afternoon. That was the thing about gentrification: Everything you moved into the neighborhood for eventually got driven out.

As he zipped down Centre Street and turned left toward Roxbury, he passed a series of looming brick tenement houses, over ten floors high, that had so far escaped change—indeed, sometimes they seemed resistant to any improvement at all. On sweet summer evenings, the Bromley Heath housing project too often turned into a battlefield where a young man slumped dead in the dirt yard or a little girl got shot in the face jumping rope in an alleyway. Murders over a whispered insult, a red shirt worn on the wrong side of a street, any one of myriad reasons that someone finds in themselves to sneak up to a man and shoot him in the back with a taped-up revolver passed down in a desperate street trade.

Ray parked in front of the projects and put the drop top back up, saying a brief prayer that no one slashed it before he returned. He walked to a side street off Columbus Avenue, stopping in front of Maleah's place, a dilapidated, gray, three-family home surrounded by an iron fence that looked near to falling down. The front porch was bursting with rubbish, an old green-painted safe, trash bags, and a pair of children's shoes. Ray lifted the latch and rang the bell at the door. A middle-aged Black woman answered: friendly eyes, slender build, dressed in white shorts and a light-colored blouse. She coddled a phone between her shoulder and cheekbone as she mixed some food in a bowl.

"Maleah?" Ray asked. She nodded almost imperceptibly. "I'm investigating a shooting that occurred at the house a few years back." Seeing her eyes narrow, he added, "Private. Not a cop."

"My family is not involved in any of that street stuff."

"Of course. This was before you got here. Involves a guy who spent some time here."

"I'ma call you back," she said, closing the phone. "Come again?"

"I'm working on a case for a guy named Sam Langford. We're looking into some new evidence. He has maintained he is innocent for years."

"I don't know that name."

"Joe Butters is involved."

"Oh, shit." She stepped outside on the porch, stealing a look back into the house.

"Can we sit down?"

She looked sheepish. "Mind if we keep our business outside here?" She looked back at the door. "I'm with someone else now. This is in the past."

He nodded. "I got it. How did you meet him?"

"We met at a Christmas party a friend invited me to at her work. He was there. I think he came with someone, a cop or something. She works for the courts. He was nice to me, I didn't know anyone there."

"How long did you date him?"

"Well, it was fast and furious. He was real nice

and sweet to begin, but then I noticed how secret he was, always texting or taking calls and closing the door. I mind my business, but after a while it got to be too much. Men who keep secrets I got no use for."

A Black man in a Celtics t-shirt came to the door and peered out with a curious look. Maleah said, "Honey, this is some old business with someone who used to live here."

He mumbled something and went back inside.

"Ahh, let's go inside then." She opened the door and led the way into a formal dining room. She offered him a seat. There were family pictures on an umber colored wall, black-and-white faces, people posed in suits and dresses, the classy standards of a bygone era. He thought of the corporate bums he saw walking around downtown Boston. Progress was an unsteady line.

"Love the old photos."

She brightened. "Old folks knew how to dress."

"Yes, they did. So, about Mr. Butters." He gave her some background on the case. "What was he doing for work then?"

"I have no idea."

"Ever discuss it?"

"I would ask. But he never say nothing. Other than he worked different jobs at some company downtown, driving and managing a bar somewhere. He didn't offer much, and I don't play the nag. He moved in with me for a while, but then the phone calls got to be too much, so I tossed him out."

"Who did he hang out with?"

"I just seen them, I never knew their names. White dudes."

"You said he was at a Christmas party. Who did he come with? You mentioned a cop."

"Yes, Irish guy. I don't know his name."

"Do you have pictures from the Christmas party?"

"You know what, that I do have." She got up, rummaged through some magazines on a table, and took out an iPad with a pink cover. After a minute, she pulled up a photo of her and Butters. "That guy in the background at the bar. That's him." She pointed to a guy with a distant look on his pale face, short hair, blue jacket. His deep-set eyes screamed cop. He seemed unaware that he was being photographed. Ray thought the man looked familiar but could not place him.

"Can I get a copy?"

"Sure." He gave her his email address, and she sent off a copy. He saw it come into his inbox and forwarded it to Robinson with a question: "Is this Magnus?"

"Can you tell me something?" Maleah asked. "Is Joey in trouble again?"

"No, not necessarily. We are piecing together his role in a case and just wanted to get your input."

She looked off into the distance. "Some guys are born into this stuff. Lying is like a second language."

"More like a first. Call me anytime if you think of anything else."

CHAPTER 6

RAY HEADED BACK to his place in the South End and spent the rest of the afternoon finishing up some reports. He decided to go see Langford again to discuss the case the next morning. He remembered Langford had complained about not having anything to read, so he went out late, walked up to the bookstore near the college dorms on Tremont, and picked out a few non-threatening titles he hoped would make it past the prison censors. An educated mind is a dangerous thing.

After traffic had settled down, he pulled out the Shelby and raced off to the prison in Walpole. In the security line, he read a poster on the wall listing the rules compiled by the prison bureaucracy. No weapons, no contraband, no writing a story for the media. Check. No black jeans, no blue jeans, no boots above the knees (except October through April). No postal uniforms or spandex. No missing buttons. No pens with springs. Books had to be cleared. No novels with gang themes or rogue sheriffs. It all made sense to someone.

Then Ray was past the sliding steel doors and walking to the attorney's rooms, where he sat and waited for prisoner W219975 to be brought forth from the cells. It was all routine now for him. As he waited, two guards escorted a prisoner wearing a belly chain, and he considered again the colossal expenditures it took to lock men away like animals. Spending those funds earlier on for more high schools or colleges may have been a better investment. Prisons were a gallery of paintings of the poor, the uneducated, the fatherless. Dispossessed men marking time to the sound of sliding steel doors as hope wilted away to the end of caring.

A sound of shaking keys. Langford walked inside. He looked at Ray across the plastic table while the guard took a chair in the lobby, sitting with hands splayed on his thighs just a few feet outside the door. Ray shut the door to the interview room as Langford sat down.

"How you doing?" Ray asked.

"Good as can be. All things considered."

"I ordered some books for you. A couple of novels, a book on pro basketball I think I mentioned earlier."

"Hey, thanks, I appreciate that. What's the hoops book?"

"The Book of Basketball. You'll love it. Ranks the '86 Celtics team as the greatest team ever."

"I need this book."

"That team had Bird in his prime. The Chief and McHale working the torture chamber down low."

"Badass."

"Yeah, I thought you'd like it. After we're done here, I'll send you a copy." Books had to arrive in original packaging, or else guards seized them as contraband.

Ray knew that guys inside appreciated any mental distraction away from the cell. Prisoners kept to the odd rhythm of the big house once they were inside. Early breakfast, some exercise, then an early lunch. Survival depended on ritual, knowing where you were supposed to be, and not running into people where you weren't.

They sat for a while, marking casual time between two people who knew that one of them had a job to do.

"I don't want to die in here," Langford said suddenly, staring at Ray. Ray recalled he had said the same thing in their first meeting. Langford's laceless sneakers squeaked on the cement as he tucked his legs under, like a child would. He sighed.

"Sam, I get it. I want to ask you about something. I saw this report about a taxi cab that was seen on Summer Street that night. Police interviewed this old Irish lady who says she saw a taxi pull over near the parking lot where the victim was found. She makes a call to the police, but during the interview she backs off that comment. Did anyone ever talk to her before trial?"

"No," Sam looked thoughtful. "We got that report late. I don't think we ever found her."

"I'll add her to the list. In fact, I'll go see her today."

"I appreciate all you're doing," Langford said, his voice thick. "People just forget we're in here. I never had anyone do something like this for me."

The men said their farewells. Ray headed to the prison parking lot and logged into the databases on his phone. He searched for Mrs. Edith Farrell. She still lived in the same apartment as before, the bottom floor of an apartment on M Street just off East 1st Street. He headed north from Walpole, looping past Blue Hill and onto the Expressway into the city. It was rarely express, and he reached Southie after an hour and parked in front of the apartment.

A light rain was falling. Ray stepped out and knocked. A woman with iron-gray hair, a knit cardigan sweater, and delicate piano hands answered the door. She looked like a school teacher from another era. She opened the door just a crack, door chain still on.

"Mrs. Farrell, sorry to bother you. I'm Ray Infantino, I'm investigating an old criminal case."

She looked him up and down and warmed to the topic. "Oh, come on in. They robbed me last week, you know, but you're dressed up nice."

Ray shrugged as he stepped inside, touching his jacket absentmindedly. Funny how people reacted to you. PI work retained a lost simplicity, the art of conversation in a cold age. You knock, they talk. Or they don't. You never knew what witness might hold the golden key.

She led him into a sunny apartment with windows thrown open to the salt air.

"What did you mean about being robbed?"

"Some kids broke into my garage," she said with a frown. "They stole tools my husband kept there. I doubt they know how to even use them."

"Sorry to hear that."

"The neighborhood is not the same."

Ray nodded, sat down in the chair opposite Mrs. Farrell, and outlined the case against Sam Langford. He brought up the report about her viewing a taxi cab near the parking lot.

"Well, I'll stop you right there. I told police about the taxi. But they didn't seem to want to listen."

"Why do you say that?"

"You know how someone keeps asking you the same questions like they think you must be wrong? That's what they did. 'How can you be sure? How can you be sure? Could you be mistaken?' One officer, I'm not sure of his name, he just kept at it. He was very rude."

"They're not known for their social niceties."

"True. Well, I am. Would you like some tea, dear?"

"Thank you."

Mrs. Farrell put a pot on the stove. Ray had her run through that night again, and she repeated the story about the taxi he had read in the report.

"What color was the cab?"

"Orange. It was orange."

"I read the police reports. The section where they cover the interview with you was very short. Just a paragraph. Says that you thought you saw a taxi but weren't sure, especially once the officer pressed you about the color."

"That's not true," she said.

Ray reached into his file. "I have a copy. It's a running report, they just kept updating it with new information. Not the best format for imparting information, which you'd think might be important for solving crimes. Would you take a look?"

"Yes, I'd like to see it." Mrs. Farrell sat down, put on reading glasses, and read for a minute until the water boiled and whistled. She fixed two cups, then went back to reading through the report. She shook her head as she put the papers down.

"I spoke to them for close to twenty minutes. I saw a cab pull over there. I told them it was orange. And they summarize what I said in a few lines? And they got it all wrong. How is that possible?" She shook her head in disgust.

"You're sure then about the color?"

"Yes."

"Are you always awake that late?"

"Yes. I don't sleep well. I stay up late and look at the TV."

Ray sat back and spread his hands on the table. "Not to question you like they did, but I have to ask—how can you be sure about the color? It was a long time ago."

"Let me show you why." Edith got up and walked to a side door, which led to a garage. Inside was a classic Mustang convertible. The car was painted burnt orange. Ray laughed out loud.

"I drive a Mustang, too."

"My husband bought this car after we got married. He only drove Fords. He painted the car himself, loved burnt orange."

"So you might remember seeing an orange car?"

"Oh, I think I would."

"Mind if I take a photo?"

"Go right ahead."

He snapped a few photos of the Mustang. If Mrs. Farrell was accurate, this would be a major piece of evidence that should have been reported to the defense. He made a note to request all records on Butters from the hackney carriage unit of the police.

Then they sat down at the kitchen table and he wrote out a declaration on a yellow pad. Edith signed it. Ray knew they were far, far away from an outcome, but this was another glimmer of hope.

It was time to push on to Joey Butters and see what he had to say about that night.

CHAPTER 7

JOEY BUTTERS RAISED his glass and gulped down his beer at the carved wooden bar inside the Hells Angels Clubhouse in Lynn. Outside the window he could see part of a death's head, the motorcycle club insignia, looming over the street like a mad dog sentinel troubling the unhappy world. There was nothing subtle about the message. The Angels descended openly in this neighborhood of scrap metal restaurants and cratered parking lots, offering the denizens the rough blessings of their trade: cheap meth and the promise of a face stomp for anyone who meddled.

Butters tipped his glass toward the club president, Frank Carmina.

"We're ready," Butters said. "Where are your guys working tomorrow?"

"They're on a project out by the waterfront. Mauro will be there, you know him. Call this number." Carmina held out his phone to show Butters the contact number.

Butters dialed the number and saved it into his phone.

"The truck will make a drop at 10 a.m. Four lawn mowers' worth." Carmina nodded and pointed to a gym bag. He kicked it open so Butters could see the wadded cash. Butters dragged it over and counted the bills.

Butters had dealt meth to the bikers for years. He arranged deliveries to certain houses in the suburbs, where a landscaping crew staffed with some club prospects were doing yard work. Butters had a guy make deliveries in bags that looked like mulch or grass seed. Between edging lawns and laying brick, the landscape crew carried the bags of meth and delivered them to a network of street sellers on the North Shore and in Boston.

Butters considered methheads a valued clientele. They got hooked quickly, and the drug was less fatal than heroin, so there was no major outcry to curtail the market. Meth addiction had downsides. The drug rotted out an addict's face and left their teeth looking like a row of tumbled gravestones. But he accepted that there were downsides to everything. His customers were devout in their passion for the pipe, smoking away their youth and limping off into a glassy twilight.

Butters had taken a role as the street face of the mob, who built on the old myths from the Troubles that Irish Catholics faced with their English over-lords. Gangsters were cast as street samurai who protected their own from the outside world. The local crews would never sell drugs in their own neighborhood, people whispered. But Butters knew it was a cynical word game: Instead, they collected rent money from street dealers who operated only with the blessing of the mob bosses. The old Irish in the neighborhoods, who hated with a special passion informers and rats, turned a blind eye to the gangs, even while drug bazaars were springing up on street corners all over the city. The occasional murder, the not-infrequent heroin overdose—these could be ignored as the mythology grew about the outlaws protecting the seaside three-deckers from the modern world.

"So tomorrow's the Winthrop route. We'll drop the tools by 8:30 a.m. at this address." He showed his phone to Carmina, who scratched something on a slip of paper. Carmina trusted paper. He hated cell phones and suspected they piped every phone conversation into a powerful government computer buried somewhere in the New Mexico desert. Carmina harbored a lot of suspicions about New Mexico; he often pointed out how rare it was that you met anyone from that state. Butters thought Carmina displayed admirable levels of paranoia.

Carmina grabbed two more beers from the bar. He led Butters toward the yard where several motorcycles sat in various states of repair.

Carmina bent down and picked up a clutch plate. "See this? The company that makes this, you call this 800 number and they replace the shit, sight unseen. You get it delivered for free." Carmina smiled and gulped his beer.

"You serious?"

"Yeah. Can you believe that shit? Sight unseen. That's why this is the greatest country on earth."

"Make money on both ends."

"I fix it, resell it, or use it myself."

"Great to be an American."

"I'll drink to that." Carmina took a swig of beer and threw the can into a barrel.

Butters liked Carmina. He was an old-school paisano from the North Shore who could certainly have been a soldier in the Mafia but took his love of bikes and crime and blazed his own way. He set up shop in Lynn as a freelance middleman for all kinds of underworld activity. He could sell anything at anytime. Tattoos writhed up and down his sinewy arms which, combined with his Sicilian blood, gave his skin a reddish hue and his nickname "Frank the Indian." By midsummer the guy looked like the spitting image of a Comanche as he rode his iron horse down the Lynnway, his bronzed arms outstretched in the summer sun. He had a brilliant cover story, Carmina did; he was among the best bike mechanics on the North Shore. Capitalizing on that reputation, Carmina moved into fencing stolen cycle and auto parts he filtered out to resellers in Rhode Island. He was an entrepreneur, with money coming in from legitimate work and also stolen merchandise. And now he did meth drops. Carmina was an earner.

Carmina and Butters walked toward the yard. "Hey, I'm hearing something about a murder case in Southie," Carmina said abruptly. "Something happening?" He held a chunk of metal, tattoos dancing on his forearms.

This caught Butters off guard. Why was Carmina bringing something like this up now? He thought for a moment before answering. "I dunno, Frank. What's this all about?"

"I got no balls in the game. But a guy I know tells me a guy he knows was approached by some PI out of Boston. Ray Infantino. He was asking this guy about you."

"Care to give a name?"

Carmina cracked a hard smile. "My guy? He's just a guy. Let's leave it at that. I'm just letting you know that someone is dropping your name in some shit."

"Okay. Well, I appreciate."

The men settled their business and Butters moved to the exit, feeling uneasy. This kind of attention could be bad for business. If this fucking private detective kept mucking around, his entire operation could be shaded. He reached the street and looked around the neighborhood before going to his car. Some kids walked by. Two Latino laborers stood at the corner, waiting for a contractor to offer them some work. He took a walk on the sidewalk, rounded a corner, and then doubled back. The street was empty. This was the price paid for the life he chose: the eternal watching, never knowing why some guy was crawling around your past. He got in his car and drove off.

CHAPTER 8

ON THE NEXT cross street, a car exited a few seconds later, carrying Ray Infantino into the river of traffic.

Butters drove fast. Ray stayed two cars behind Butters and tracked him back to Route 99 near Charlestown. Traffic was slowing down as the roads merged near Charlestown. He lost Butters on the Charlestown Bridge and watched as he eased through a red light and disappeared into the North End.

Ray made a few runs down Atlantic Street to find Butters but came up empty. He checked the address he had pulled up for Butters in databases and drove into the warren of narrow streets that led into the heart of the North End. He parked next to a hydrant on Fleet Street, got out, and stepped into the vestibule of the building. There was no one named Butters on the mailbox. Ray rang a doorbell to the top floor, but no one answered.

He decided to sit on the place for a bit. The sidewalks were narrow and the brick three-deckers loomed over the street. A delivery truck rumbled by and double parked, blocking all traffic for five minutes. Drivers honked. The trucker shrugged and hauled his wares to the restaurants lining the street.

No one came or went from the building. Ray decided to return later.

He drove across town with the sun dropping on the horizon, where the light seemed intent on slashing the eyes of passersby. It was that evening time when the city caught its breath and stretched its workaday legs, ready to release men and women from their professional masks and into cafes and bars where they donned some new costume they chose for the night.

As he approached the South End, a police cruiser pulled up behind him, blue lights twinkling in the rearview. Ray pulled over to the curb. A husky older cop got out, ruddy cheeks running to a delta of damaged capillaries. He looked a bit unready for the job. He waddled to the door.

"Good afternoon," Ray said.

"License and registration," came the monotone reply.

Ray opened the glove compartment. He wondered if he ever kept gloves in there as he sifted through discarded electronics and Dunkin Donuts napkins that seemed to have collected there for years.

"Do you know why I stopped you?" The big man rose on tiptoes.

"I don't. Enlighten me."

The cop paused, testing for safe levels of mockery. "Tint too dark."

Ray handed him the papers. "I have a PI license. The tint is legal." The cop looked at him, none too happy now, took the papers, and returned to his cruiser. Just one of those afternoons when bird shit falls on your head and everyone else seems to laugh.

The cop came back a minute later. He handed back the documents. "Have a good one, Mr. Infantino." Ray scanned the officer's badge. He was tempted to get the number and report the guy, but he let it go. Time to move on.

Back at the office, his secretary Sheri looked up as he entered. She was working late shredding old files that had been unearthed when they moved to a new space. She had arranged the first floor for client meetings while Ray was living in the rooms above. Sheri had been with him since the beginning, and although she was now a grandmother, she had no intention of retiring.

"You just got an unusual message from a Mr. Robinson. He called and said Butters is living at 297 North Street."

Ray smiled. "That would be retired Detective Robinson of Boston PD. Cops can be blunt, we know that." He took the message slip. "Thanks."

"You ever think of being a police officer? You would look good in blue."

"Too narrow. Plus they wouldn't appoint me chief on day one of my employment."

"They have nice gadgets."

"So do we. And I don't have a union telling me I can't fire bums who don't know how to use the gadgets."

"I'm sure you'd find a way, dear."

For the rest of the evening, Ray wrote up reports on the big civil cases that kept the business flowing, and the minor cases he picked up out of interest or a sense of helping the right guy push back against the other side. One of the great joys of self-employment: the end-of-the-month whale hunt for late-paying customers. He put on some classical music and let it play until he finished.

Evening drew on, and Ray looked out the window at the sky: It was time to try Butters again. Butters wasn't a health club kind of guy so he might be back home. He slipped a small, green reporter's notebook into the inside pocket of his navy blue blazer. He headed to the Red Line subway, watching the multitude of faces—brown, black, and white—pancaked between oversized headphones, faces grinning, grimacing, bored. Crisp women in business suits, college slobs in torn shorts and flip flops. He took a seat and leaned forward to avoid the shoulder-smashing dance with riders on the plastic seats. He closed his eyes and drifted into a rolling reverie as the subway car clacked on to the station.

Dusk was blotting out the star-pricked sky when he got off at the Aquarium and walked through Christopher Columbus Park to the address he had for Butters. Ray walked up the granite slab sidewalk between the merchant buildings, the faded names of long-dead businesses still flecking off the brick. Ray worried about Butters. He needed the bastard to talk. He would be irritated if the man showed no balls and refused him.

Ray got to North Street and walked by two old men in guayabera shirts sitting in lawn chairs below the streetlights. They commandeered several parking spots with the chairs, turning it into an asphalt patio. Not exactly in the middle of the street, that would be crass, but there was a street-level message being delivered. It said, we still matter in this place. This was what the old timers did in the North End, dyed in the traditional ways. They preferred the street circus, measuring out their time with cigars and opulent gestures, sitting on stoops filled with neighbors, preferring the living pulse of the streets instead of the cramped freedom of a cell phone.

Ray nodded at the old men as they talked.

"Freddie, these kids, I dunno."

"Please. Don't say it."

"This generation, what do they call them, millennial?" The man brushed his chin with his fingers. "I say to you: douchebags. The pussification of America."

Ray paused on the sidewalk near Butters' place to check his notes.

"My mother told us, always remember, no one's better than you. But you're no better than anyone, either. These guys, they come out of college and expect three square a day, a job on mahogany row. And a fancy title. *Madonne.*"

Freddie nodded. "I hear these guys talking, they don't know how to please a woman."

His friend laughed.

"It's all screwed up now. Equal rights, equal this, equal that. Christ, most of these young guys eat out their girlfriends on the first date."

"Please. I know this. We used to say, take care of it yourself."

"They eat 'em like a box lunch," Freddie said, nodding his head. He crossed his feet, sat back, and took a deep puff on his cigar.

Ray felt immensely better about the night as he walked toward the vestibule of Butters' apartment. The door was locked. He waited a minute until he saw a young woman coming down; he smiled, nodded, and stepped by her without a glance as she held the door. When it came to getting into buildings, it paid to dress well.

Butters lived on the top floor, rear side. Ray knocked and heard a stirring within. "Who is it?"

"Joe, this is Ray Infantino here."

"Who?"

"I'm investigating an old criminal case."

Butters made some protestations.

"Please, I just need a minute, it won't take long. It's something you should know about."

Ray looked on as the door swung open. A man

stuck out a worn face tattooed with more bad times than good. His eyebrows were scarred over like a boxer's and a long gash ran from the right side of his mouth, as if someone had tried to carve a jack-o'-lantern into his face. He seemed more a bag of bones than a living man, all shoulders and bony wrists and sharp eyes, skin taut from something other than exercise. Drug skinny. But his eyes were clear. Perhaps the look was a remnant of old debaucheries.

"So, Joey, let's sit down, it won't take a minute," Ray said as he stepped over the threshold without being invited.

If he cared, Butters made no comment. He just moved to a nearby table and sat in the chair as if expecting the worst. "So what is it now?"

It was clear Butters had had more than an occasional visit from a detective. That was interesting. Ray tried to gauge Butters' mood. "Do you remember the Sam Langford case?"

"Who?"

"You remember the case? You testified."

"Wait, who you working for? Him?"

"Yes, he has an appeal."

"Ahhhh," he grimaced. "I shouldn't talk to you."

"It might save some time down the road if this goes to trial."

Butters thought about that and gave a half-hearted shrug. "How long's this gonna take?"

"Just a few questions. I know it's been a long time."

"Yeah, what, over ten years?"

"A girl at the bar, the Electric House, was killed that night."

Butters sat back and rubbed his mouth. "Yeah, I remember."

"There is an appeal being filed."

"There always is."

"True. But this one might win."

"Well, good luck to him. I gotta tell you, I remember nuthin'."

Ray just looked at him. "It would mean a lot if you would."

"I'm sorry. But I got jumped a few years ago, there by the Quiet Man Pub. Got a concussion. You can get the records."

"Not so quiet there, huh?"

"Not after midnight. Yuppies are fuckin' the place up."

"Yes, they are. God bless us all," Ray said, looking around at the apartment. *Try a different angle.* The kitchen was spotless in an antiseptic way that suggested a lack of activity rather than diligence. There was a poster showing Bruins superstar Bobby Orr making his iconic icy leap into history during the 1970 Stanley Cup.

"That picture never gets old," Ray said.

Butters looked over and nodded. "Oh yeah, I'll always remember that."

"There's fame. And then there's that level of fame. Orr hasn't bought a drink in this town since."

"Back when we were kids!" Butters nodded.

"Hockey in the seventies was the balls," said Ray. He watched as Butters settled into his chair a bit. "Anyway, I'm hoping you can paint some detail in for me. Please." Ray removed a notebook and pen from his jacket pocket. "Can you tell me anything you saw and heard? Might help this guy."

"I barely remember this."

"Well, you testified, right?"

"God, it's been so long." said Butters. He picked at his shirt. "You're working for Langford, but how do you beat this case now?"

"We're looking into a few things about some of the cops."

Butters looked around the room a bit as if a ladder might drop from the sky to lift him out. "Listen, I got nothing against the guy…" he trailed off. "I told you, my memory. And I had a rough life, doing drugs and on the run."

"On the run. But I'm in your living room."

"Well, that's true." Butters clammed up.

"I told you, I'm not a cop."

Ray sat and watched Butters avoid looking at him. Typical fuckmop; most of these guys crapped themselves when you pressed them. As Neil Robinson had described, Butters was putty for someone to shape, that was clear.

"I saw in the transcript that you saw Langford out by the waterfront late. And you knew him from the neighborhood."

"Mmm, hmm, yeah."

"What were you doing that night?"

"I don't remember."

"Police talk to you?"

"Yeah."

"Why?"

"I was coming home late." He stopped again and looked away.

"What did you see that night?"

"I don't really think I saw much. I saw a guy walking."

"Were you coming from work, or something?"

"I forget."

"How did Magnus first come talk with you?" Ray looked at him. "He was not lead detective. But he ended up running the entire investigation, right?"

Butters shrugged. "Came up in the same neighborhood as most of the guys he arrested. Had the street knowledge, the intel."

"And the leverage."

Butters nodded. "Sure."

"You're all in the same business in the end, right?"

"You could say that."

"Some things you do, they can't be taken back."

"If you say so." Butters took a swig of beer. "You know, I can't go there. There are things that were done," he trailed off. "You have no idea. You fuck with them, shit happens. All of a sudden you get arrested. You catch a new case. Your girlfriend's kids get picked up by DCF. Somehow, everything you do is known to them and you're on the express lane to fuckville. That era, the gangs had people everywhere—city hall, the police, the unions. Might as well change their logo to a fuckin' shamrock with a pistol."

"Anything recent happen with you?"

"Look, I know what you gotta do. But there are people in this town who never walked right after crossing them. When these guys took over, forget it," Butters said as he shook his head.

"Who?"

Butters lifted a finger and pointed to the Bruins poster. "Even Bobby would know not to go there."

Ray looked around the apartment, just another overpriced rat hole in the North End. He lobbed a few more questions at Butters, who saw a way out of this awkwardness and gave snippets of information. Ray led him on a slow dance and got nothing. Then he sat back and put away his notebook. Butters fell for it and looked relieved.

"Given this guy is innocent, what do you think should happen to someone who may have lied during that trial?"

Butters seemed surprised at this turn and, for the first time, a look of something other than slovenly disinterest flitted across his brow. He shrugged.

"Langford has a sister, a father. They talk on Sundays when the family goes to see him at the prison. Trying to keep it all together. Helluva thing to do to a man."

Butters shifted in his seat. "Prison is tough on the family."

"Yes, it is. Well, the truth always surfaces in the end, right?" He shifted gears again. "How long did you drive a cab?"

Butters' corpse-like pallor took on a deeper shade of pale. Ray looked at him with renewed interest.

"Why do you ask that?"

"Orange colored cab."

Butters said nothing.

"There was a note in the court record on this point." Ray stopped talking and let Butters cook for a bit.

Butters roused himself. "Well, I did drive a cab a long time back. But it was a big outfit, Metro Cab."

"You sure?"

"Pretty sure. They had yellow taxis."

"That's all right. The hackney unit will have that information, anyway," Ray said. He looked away out the window and returned his eyes to Butters. "Ever drive a gypsy cab? You know, unmarked, not official."

"Not that I can remember." Butters looked away.

"Burnt orange?"

Butters said nothing.

"The girl who was killed, she had a friend with her that night. Did you take her friend to the hotel that night?"

At this, Butters looked startled. He licked his lips and picked at something on his shirt. He made a move to get up.

Ray was fishing here—had not seen any evidence in the file to show that Butters worked as a gypsy cab driver that night. But if he drove that night, it explained a lot of things.

"She was seen inside an orange taxi. You know the color."

"No, no, not familiar to me." Butters looked as if he had seen a ghost.

Ray questioned him for a while longer but Butters slipped into a funk and gave him clipped answers. Ray got up to leave.

"So what's gonna happen?" Butters asked.

"We have a long way to go. I'll be in touch as this thing develops. Keep you posted."

* * *

Butters got out of the chair, his face downcast. He didn't say goodbye as Ray stepped out the door. Christ, nothing good happened when you answered the doorbell these days.

Butters moved to the front window that overlooked the street. A minute later, he watched as the PI left the front door. He felt the guy's presence still in the apartment, the placid, dusty air disturbed now by something unexpected, like an afterimage of sharp light. The PI showed a calm manner, relaxed even, but behind that his eyes had been searching all over and through, not asking permission. This guy looked like a driver, a plugger, someone who would push and push. Butters felt it.

What a day, this old case coming up like a skeleton in a flooded graveyard.

Butters let out a deep breath, walked to the refrigerator, and got a beer. Then he sat in the chair and took a long drink as he looked out over the rooftops.

The past was never far away in Boston. For an American city, it was old. Everywhere you looked, there were aged things, pockmarked brick sidewalks, old graveyards with tombstones carved with winged death's-heads; it spooked him when he was a kid and saw those stone avenging angels.

Night fell outside the window. Voices rose from the sidewalks, boisterous crowds on Hanover pushing into the restaurants for supper. He thought back to his childhood, living in the old row houses, growing up with McBain and Magnus and the other Irish kids in Southie. He thought back to what he once was, what they all had been so many years ago. Those hot summer nights, everyone young and ferocious, their futures stretching out over the limitless Atlantic horizon.

He had been a good soldier all these years. Loyalty was a bramble path, and the rewards grew greater with time. But for too many years, that night with Langford on the waterfront gnawed his gut. Now it was coming back again. A ghost on the waterfront that never let him rest.

PART 2

VARIOUS SCENES

1989-2013

CHAPTER 9

August 14, 1989, Truro Beach

MUSCLES STRAINING, THE fishmonger yanked the last case of seafood out of his North End shop and loaded it onto the truck. This was a major delivery for a weekend. He had woken early to prepare for the trip down the Cape. He played that word over his tongue as he drove that morning; it sounded like paradise compared to the city squalor he saw each day, five kids sleeping in a room and crap floating in Boston Harbor you wouldn't touch with a stick.

Two hours later, he arrived at an enormous farmhouse on the outer Cape. The house overlooked the ocean, isolated from its neighbors by sand dunes and deep stands of beach grass. He didn't ask questions about the owner. He had been told the guests here would include mafioso from the old neighborhood. Even the boss was rumored to be making an appearance. That was enough for him. Curiosity, they say, killed the cat. So he didn't meow.

The fishmonger rumbled up the dirt driveway toward the house. He could see cars pulled up close near the house: Cadillacs, Buicks, big American cars. A few men in dark suits. He recognized Joey "Shanks" Barboza; they grew up together on Prince Street. He dressed real good for a weekend, a nice silk shirt and a suit. There was a major party going on. Or maybe someone died.

He pulled around to the back of the house, as he had been told. He got out and knocked at the rear door. Through the window, he could see a large, modern kitchen, pots dangling from a hood above a commercial stove. Very nice setup. The cook came out and looked over the haul, made certain that everything was fresh. Shrimps, scallops, anchovies for the Caesar salad, monkfish, tuna, swordfish. $1,300 worth of seafood. The cook paid him cash, counting out the bills while chewing the end of a cigarette.

The fishmonger drove away from the house. He came upon a curve in the road. Up ahead, a state trooper parked on the side of the road. He slowed down. He noticed more cruisers parked down the road. A roadblock. He turned around and drove back to the house, sweat pouring off his brow.

Somehow, word of the police presence had already reached the farmhouse. A group of men in dress pants and shirts ran out of the farmhouse and steamed through the beach grass. The cops were driving up the dirt driveway and tearing out of the cars after the fleeing men.

He couldn't believe what he was seeing. The scene looked comical: dozens of big men in dress shirts plowing through grass in loafers as they hightailed it toward the beach. Some guys ran fast like they were real athletes. One big guy, face red as a boiled lobster, crashed into the ground. No one stopped to help him. Some guys made for a clump of pines. It was clear the cops were unprepared for the sheer numbers; one trooper was on the radio shouting for help. The fishmonger sat in his truck, not sure where to go. He wondered what might happen to all the seafood.

When the dust cleared, twelve Mafia members were arrested on various charges. The word filtered out to the streets: Once again, someone had tipped off the cops to a major sit-down. A rat was loose, a rat that chewed up the Italian Mafia but left the other gangs alone.

CHAPTER 10

Summer 1997, South Boston

IT WAS EARLY in the afternoon and the Electric House Pub was rocking full force—construction workers, longshoreman, a scattering of women Tommy McBain liked to refer to as dishrag whores. The building was all cement and glass blocks. No one could see in, no one could get out. Capacity was sixty. Triple that number pressed against the walls.

McBain was a mid-level boss with the South Boston crew. He perched at the rear bar, drinking boilermakers as the afternoon flooded away. AC/DC pounded from the jukebox. Amid the wailing of Angus' guitar, some notions were running through in his head.

This was the summer of the gang wars. The feds obsessed over La Cosa Nostra, and after a series of arrests, the playing fields were wide open. The South Boston crew, a Dorchester group of mixed ethnics—Italians, Puerto Ricans, Jewish bookies—had absorbed the remnants of Old Colony, an older, weaker gang that had originated from the housing projects off D Street in Southie. There were a few rogue groups still stepping out of line and in need of a sharp lesson. The previous month, one of the renegade members of Old Colony, Peter Cunningham, was shot while walking by the power plant. A car pulled up; a man leaned out and unloaded a shotgun blast into the fatback of his legs. Cunningham lay writhing in pain for a half hour until someone found him lying in a pool of blood.

Retaliation for the ambush took place a day later. Someone gunned down a South Boston soldier named Ralph Gigante on Castle Island as he walked along the shore. Gigante survived and led a retaliatory raid just one cool month later. It was a professional job. Gigante saw no need to rush out angry and bawling in the street like a movie gangster. So he tinkered with electronics and set up a remote control pipe bomb beneath a car parked at the home of an Old Colony captain. He stepped inside the next morning and Gigante, watching from a block away, set off the bomb. The captain's legs were blown off, his torn flesh speckled red along a white fence running along the driveway. Gigante joked about making Irish stew; he was a funny bastard.

Lance Collins, the boss of Old Colony, called for a meeting with the South Boston crew—there was no way they could survive a loss ratio like this. He had fewer men to start, and the bombings were unnerving.

He called for the carnage to end and agreed to cede control of the few smuggling routes they still owned. As captain of the crew that operated the lucrative waterfront rackets, Tommy McBain came into his greatest coup, inheriting the wharf area controlled by Old Colony.

McBain's crew also had help from an unexpected ally. The FBI office in Boston was populated with several agents from Southie, many of whom grew up in the housing projects near the harbor. These housing projects spawned cops and criminals in equal measure, boys who never left the old playground rivalries and raced off in different directions; some to law enforcement, some to the gangs. Sometimes, these old connections could make a man some extra money. The FBI's Upper Echelon Informant Program was geared to one thing: prosecuting the Mafia. Mob cases generated fantastic press. The Mafia captured the public's imagination as the face of underground crime: blood oaths, swarthy faces, secret ceremonies where swarthy men burned pictures of saints.

So a deal was made: If McBain's crew fed law enforcement intelligence on the Mafia, they were free to operate without interference. So long as they avoided involvement in violent crime and murder, the arrangement would work.

As time passed, McBain observed a ravenous hunger behind the eyes of his federal overseers. The feds needed convictions at any cost. And the gangsters knew it. It was best to just feed the beast. As time went on, the line between cop and criminal grew murkier as the bosses concluded that the agency now needed the gangsters more than the gangsters needed the feds.

The old vigilance over not dealing with shooters fell away. When key witnesses began to disappear from the streets of Boston, the feds made only half-hearted inquiries. McBain's crew offered shrugs and dangled more leads into La Cosa Nostra. The beaches of South Boston turned into midnight burial grounds. McBain and his crew realized there was no marker between the gangsters and the cops anymore. It was open season. The gang prospered, moving into new rackets such as smuggling weapons to the Irish Republican Army for the freedom fight. McBain came up with an Irish solution: shipping weapons inside coffins to avoid customs agents. Soon, Irish-American corpses sent across the sea for burial in old Cork County soil kept their ancestral silence next to rifles that McBain's crew packed in their stiff hands.

Tonight, McBain's men would celebrate a successful heist in grand style. A shipment of Guinness had come in on the freighter *Valinor*, out of Dublin. The crew got their land legs by noon and McBain saw that the beer flowed and the waitresses brushed up to the men.

He walked back to his office where the captain, a third-generation sailor out of Cork County, was making sure the paperwork was in place and marking up beer deliveries to different pubs. The Bat Cave on Canal Street would take delivery on a half order and send the rest back as skunked.

McBain worked the phone on some other projects. He knew a guy who ran numbers at Triples. The guy assured him that there would be a fire at a pub on Dot Ave in two days exactly. All part of an insurance bust-out. Some of the booze would get lost, while the rest got sold out the back door. Then the place would burn.

"Make sure the invoice shows delivery by 5 p.m. today," McBain said. "Double up on the stock. Cause it goes out the door the night before."

"I'll make the change. Always a pleasure coming to the States," the pockmarked captain said. McBain shook the guy's hand. Made in America.

Around 8 p.m., McBain limped out of his office into the smokey gloom at the bar. It was going to be a weekend to remember. The boys were flush with cash from the weekly book, the booze scams, the gun smuggling overseas. Two of the boys were driving down to Wollaston Beach the next day to buy a new Buick Riviera. Cash deal, thank you very much. This was how a poor man banked: buying a big American car.

The far wall flashed a wedge of light as the front door opened. Two young girls came inside. They took seats at the bar. McBain watched them for a bit. Nice girls, the usual pairing. Jesus, what were they doing here? The quiet one, cute in a shy way that appealed to certain men. Not him, though. He had his eye on the second girl. A blonde with the complete package, an angelic mouth that inspired obscene fantasies in him the second he looked her over. She had probably convinced her doe-eyed friend to slum in old Southie, see some colonial-era history, but they had no idea where they were going. No one just wandered into the Electric House. They weren't working girls, their look was too clean.

McBain wondered what kind of taxi driver would let two lambs out by a volcano like this place. He slid off the stool, pulled his belt up, and sauntered over to get close to them.

CHAPTER 11

THE TWO GIRLS, Katie Donnegan and Emily Johansen, traveled from Rhode Island to Boston to visit various historic sites. "We were at Faneuil Hall, and we took a cab to Castle Island. And the driver dropped us off here for a drink."

"This is the last outpost of decency."

Katie laughed, glancing over the scars that snaked down Tommy McBain's forehead, a tale of brawls won and lost. They chatted a bit and drinks came and emptied. Everyone got rowdier in the bronze light of the bar. McBain got up to go to the office and leaned into the bartender, Jimmy Sales.

"Keep it flowing over there."

An hour later, even the quiet one, Emily, had come out of her hole. Everyone was chatting, plastered on the cheap beer. Emily's head swayed a bit, and she stopped from time to time to wipe her mouth with the back of her hand. True to her roots, Katie was holding up much better despite her lean frame.

She caught this Tommy McBain staring at her a bit. He directed a few smiles at her, very much the gentleman farmer, shepherding drinks and sending whiskey shots around the table. She liked him. He was tough in all the good ways, charming.

As it got close to midnight, Katie noticed Emily had almost passed out. She rested her head on her arms. Some guys were coming to the table, bantering and joking with their friend McBain.

"I need to take her to the ladies' room," Katie said. She grabbed Emily's arm and shook her awake. Emily's head lurched up. Katie walked her friend to the bathrooms.

McBain finished his beer. "I'm gonna get them a ride back to their hotel," McBain said to the bartender.

"Oh, Tommy boy, take me along!"

McBain shot him a tight grin.

The girls emerged from the ladies' room with Emily dragging her feet and stumbling.

"We gotta leave," Katie said.

"Hey, no problem, I'll give you a lift downtown."

"I think we should take a cab," Katie said. "She's wasted." Katie had an iciness in her voice. She didn't blame him for Emily drinking her ass off, but now she had to deal with it. She was not happy.

"You sure? Trying to get a cab down here after midnight—" McBain threw up his hands. She objected, but he cut her off. "Hey, no problem. I'll have them call from the bar. It'll be a few minutes."

He walked over to the bar where the beer flowed

and ardent political discussions were punctuated with loud laughs.

Katie watched McBain make a quick phone call. She tended to her friend and kept an eye out on the street. Then she saw the lights of an orange-colored taxi pull to the curb.

Katie walked Emily out to the street. The smell of saltwater was strong tonight. Emily's eyes were almost closed as she staggered along.

"Let me help her in," McBain said.

Katie hesitated, then nodded. "Yes, thanks."

The cab was an old Chevy painted a burnt orange. She saw rust spotting the bottom of the doors and CHARLES RIVER in faded white letters on the door. Hard rock thudded from the speakers. McBain said something to the driver, and the taxi sped off.

The driver headed deeper into Southie. Katie watched as her friend's head lolled on the headrest. She looked around the cab and noticed there was no meter. Weird. Probably a friend of the guys at the pub. Whatever, as long as it was a legitimate taxi. Passing headlights illuminated the driver's face from time to time as they passed through the streets—a thick-lipped Irish mug peered back at her.

She noticed the lights of the downtown towers were fading in the distance.

She looked into the rearview mirror a minute later and caught the driver's eyes in a slit of light on his face, crinkled like he was mulling over a private little joke.

"Excuse me, but I think we're going the wrong way."

More hard rock pounded from the radio. The driver said nothing. She tried to roll down the window, but the lever didn't work. *Start screaming*, she thought. But out the window, she saw only a hulking structure and empty lots. There was no one around. Thick charcoal lines of smokestacks loomed through the night sky.

The driver pulled left off the street, and she saw a sign, Summer Street. He wheeled into an empty lot past a long brick wall. Down a long path, she could see the sea rippling outside the window.

"Why are we stopping?" She reached for her phone.

The driver gazed back at her, eyes flitting over her face as if looking for something to seize on.

Then a car pulled in back of the cab. A figure got out, a darker shadow against a mass of trees. The taxi driver rolled down the window.

"Take a hike, Butters," said a voice—Katie recognized Tommy from the bar.

"Wait a minute!" she shouted.

Her friend was a dead lump in the seat. The driver mumbled something, got out of the car, then walked off into the night.

Tommy stepped into the driver's side and jerked the car into gear, creeping deep into the empty terminal lot. Katie screamed. Fear flooded her belly. Tommy parked and in one motion, he was over the seat and on top of her. He grabbed her face, hunted for her mouth, kissing her roughly. She moved her head toward the floor, trying to break his steel grip. She gouged his face and tried pushing him off. A stench of cigarette smoke, old leather, and something else, some primitive thing just beyond the senses, the smell of blood or something worse.

She saw Emily at the outskirts of her vision, still passed out. *Jesus, wake up here.* No one coming. Tommy reared up over her. *Oh, God, not this.*

Nowhere to go.

She tried to fight back, but he pinned back her arms. His neck was close, the stink of his bristles flooding her senses. She heard him groan as he turned his head to one side.

Katie bit him full on, teeth sinking into the pink flesh of his lower lip.

McBain roared in pain, rearing back. Blood ran from his lip. He punched the girl hard, once, twice. Then he lost it, drilling hard shots into her body there, there, there.

Katie put up no resistance anymore. Something was wrong in her belly. It hurt in a thick, warm way. She dissolved down into the seat and all sounds grew distant and gray.

CHAPTER 12

THE CAR SHOOK with a kind of animal fury. Then it stopped. McBain felt the mad tide ebbing out.

He sat back for a minute and closed his eyes. Time passed. A minute? Ten? He was spent. Then he opened his eyes. He looked around the car and stared at the girl, a soft thing that was once a face.

"Jesus." Deep down, he knew she was hurt bad. There had to be something he could do. He had really let it go this time. Not good. But the little thing bit a chunk of flesh off him, hadn't she? And that wasn't the thing to do when ol' Tommy was having a spell of it. He touched his neck and felt a minor scratch. This was getting a bit out of control. A girl half-naked on the seat. Another one passed out next to her.

Then he looked out past the decaying brick wall. No one was in the yard. Sidewalks running into the distance, empty, quiet. Offshore, ship lights glowed over the gasoline waters of the harbor. He got out of the car and adjusted his pants. Then he opened the trunk. Oily rags, beer cans, tire irons, a jacket, an old green Celtics t-shirt. He took the shirt out. He got back in the car and wiped her face down. It would not do for a piece of Tommy-boy to be in her teeth now, would it? He held her mouth open and cleaned her up as best he could. There was a half-empty coffee mug on the floor, and he dabbed the cotton in there and wiped her face. Then he tore off a second rag and wiped down his face.

McBain knew he was facing a critical moment. He looked again at Katie. She wasn't moving at all. He reached over and lifted her wrist almost tenderly. There was no pulse—nothing. He sat for a while in the darkness.

He saw a cell phone on the front seat. Whose was it? He thought for a moment which phone would be best to use, weighing the options. Then he picked up the phone, called Butters, and told him what to do.

McBain got out and looked around again. There was a clump of dying hedges near the entrance gate. He got into the car and drove alongside a hedge. A rat scurried through the grass. All quiet on the water-front. He hoisted the girl over his shoulder—she was so light, like a sack of rags. He trudged through the darkness to the debris-strewn berm near the entry gate. He lowered her to the ground and dragged her by her arms behind some shrubs. He felt good, calm. That pleased him—he had the icy control to do this thing. It had been an accident, after all. He never intended this.

McBain jammed her knees up and propped her on her side. Her top was open and her full breasts fell to one side. Her skin was bruising a reddish purple. He pulled her blouse closed, tucked it in, covered her up. When he finished, he crouched down and loped back to the car.

Goddamn, right on the night when the boys were peaking, cash flowing, all this was going to shit over a dead girl.

A car drove down Summer Street and pulled over some ways down the street. He saw a figure get out and walk toward him with a distinctive, off-kilter gait—Butters. McBain pulled out, drove the car to Sea Street, and parked under the maples.

Butters walked up to the car. He looked in the rear seat and his face twitched. "Jesus, Tommy. Where's the other one?"

McBain stepped out and pulled him into the shadows below the trees.

"Never mind that," he said quietly. "You're gonna take this one back downtown. You saw her friend go off with a guy. Remember?" He snapped Butters with a flat look. "She wanted to go to some other bars." He gestured to the girl in the backseat. "This one's not gonna remember a fucking thing. And phone records will show she called the cab."

Butters looked down at his feet and rubbed his face. He looked around and kicked a crushed can in the gutter. "Okay, Tommy. Whatever you say, man."

McBain moved close to Butters and absorbed

his space. He put his hand on Butters' shoulder and gazed at his eyes, spider-webbed in red, as usual.

"I'll do your remembering for you. Remember this: You took her back. Her friend went AWOL with a guy out of the bar. That's what you saw." McBain gave Butters a hard slap on the back. "Beautiful night."

A smell of decaying fish drifted from the harbor. The moon back-lit the beams of the gantry cranes, arms stretching across the water. They watched as a figure walked up the street from Summer Street. McBain recognized him. A guy who came in the Electric House occasionally for a brew, but more often just walked the neighborhood. He thought for a moment. Langford was the name.

McBain stood and watched Langford walking toward the beach.

"See that guy?" he said to Butters.

"Yeah."

"He was at the pub tonight with the other girl. Take a good look at him. Then we'll talk."

Butters got in the taxi. McBain slid past a chain-link fence down a path, and disappeared from sight.

CHAPTER 13

FOR TWO DAYS, delivery trucks roared past the gate near the channel. Dust clouds danced in their wake while the disembodied arms of cranes rotated slowly through the sky overhead, dangling freight trailers like a metallic child playing with Matchbox cars. The long days of August, summer humidity holding down the pungent fish smell until it felt like scales coated your skin.

Emily had woken the next morning at the hotel. Katie was missing. She called the police immediately and reported her missing friend. But the police told her no one was legally missing after just twenty-four hours in Boston. People disappeared all the time in the city—into a lover's bed in the South End, passed out near the river in a clump of bushes, holed up in an apartment in Providence until the next vampire night out in search of drugs or other distractions.

Mid-morning on the third day, a truck driver noticed something was malfunctioning with his brakes. He slowed just inside the gate. The driver got out to have a look. Jesus, something smelled nasty. An odor peeling off the sea, a rottenness that was akin to dead fish, but worse. He walked to a brownish clump of bushes—old cans, cigarette butts, coffee cups. Then he saw something else behind, bloated and purplish. Jetsam from the sea. But when he took a closer look into the hedge, a swollen face peered out, tongue protruding, and he shouted then, gesturing wildly—the hell with the delivery, there was a dead body over here.

Soon the boys in blue were crawling all over the yard, looking for evidence. Two detectives in blazers arrived, sweating in the sun and talking to witnesses. They called Emily to come downtown to make the identification on the body. An officer picked her up and drove to the morgue. She walked through a marble lobby decorated with two sphinxes, complete with Egyptian headdresses, hunched at the entrance to the basement. Inside, the dank tiled walls glistened with formaldehyde and the passing of a thousand souls. She looked inside the sliding locker at the body and burst into uncontrollable sobs. After she regained some sense of control, two burly cops sat down with her.

"The guys at the bar, they know something."

McBain got a tip from a cop on his payroll that they were coming. He was ready.

The ballgame burbled from the TV. The boys were shooting pool and drinking. The bartender poured shots and beers. McBain made it a point to be there all day, just like he always was. If they had questions, he would be at the bar. He was very findable. A citizen going about his day. The cut on his face was healing. It would not be noticed.

Two plainclothes detectives came by at just after 3:00 p.m., one a Mick named Robinson, who McBain recognized from the projects in Southie. The other was a young kid, darker, maybe Latino from Jamaica Plain or East Boston. What was happening to this city? Cop work belonged to the Irish.

"This girl, she was here with a friend two nights past," McBain said, pointing at her photo. The crack of balls came from the billiards table behind him. Jimmy McD was knocking off all comers on the table. But the pauses between shots grew longer than usual, and everyone was tight as wire. A low hum of concentration. Walt Riddick sat his brawny frame at the end of the bar and made no attempt to hide his disdain. *Fuck these blue clowns coming in here. They ain't gonna get a scrap.* Patrons were peering out of their eye slits at McBain and the cops, waiting for a signal for which way this little dance was going to go.

"What time?"

"Not sure, but they were here most of the night. Pretty girls. What happened?"

Robinson ignored the question. "You talk with her?"

"Just a bit. Had a drink, said hello."

"What'd you talk about?"

"Nothing really. Just a few words on the way to the shitter."

Riddick snickered. Robinson looked over at him but said nothing, just a flat-eyed glare than ran all over Riddick. McBain could see that Robinson would be a real prick if pushed. Best to give him a bit of rope.

"Look, these gals were out of their element. Obviously. We all kept an eye out, made some small talk. They had a nice time. She and some guy got a cab at the end of the night."

"What color was the cab?"

"I'm not sure. Dark-colored, I think."

"Did you sit next to her?"

"Yeah, I think so."

"What did you talk about?"

"Things boys and girls talk about at bars."

"Which is what?"

"I forget."

"You know their names?"

"Nah. One of them was hammered."

"Who?"

"Her friend." He tapped the picture of the girl. "Some of the guys held the door. They went out and were gone."

"So you touched her." Robinson just said this, not really a question.

"Not sure. Just wanted to help." He looked at Robinson. "Any gent would do that, right? You know how these college girls drink now."

"Who called the taxi?"

"Not sure."

"Was it you?"

"Nah."

"You remember the driver?"

"Nah."

"We have a witness from the hotel who says an orange taxi took her there. You see an orange cab that night?"

"Not that I recall."

Robinson bent his head as if looking under McBain's chin.

"Look, that night was nothing to remember. Just another night."

"Except a girl walks into this piss shack and ends up dead on the waterfront." Robinson leaned toward him. "Right, Tommy. Just another night."

McBain just folded his hands like he was praying to a higher power. "We saw them out. It was all we could do. Why hassle me?"

McBain looked around at the lean, sullen faces. Their hatred for the cops rose up in waves; he could feel it. These were his people, sons born to hard-bitten ironworkers and first-generation Irish girls. Some were hard men who disappeared for weeks at a time to work the shady side of the street up and down the east coast. They had picked up his signal. Information was running dry for the rest of the night.

Robinson frowned. "Thanks, Tommy. Let me know if you hear of anything. I know a guy like you wouldn't want a turd who would do this thing in here anyway."

"You got that right."

Robinson leaned in, staring. "There's a cut on your face."

"Musta cut it shaving."

"I'll be wanting a blood sample."

"Get a warrant." He knew it was nothing to worry about, small as it was. His men were locked down now; they knew the fight was over. Some J.J. Cale came on the radio and brought a Tulsa slow-down to the proceedings. The bartender wiped down the wood and poured out beers for Riddick and the rest. Robinson and his partner turned back on the place and the pool game returned to a more natural pace. The cops walked out.

"You got jack-shit," muttered Tommy. He picked up his beer and yelled for the bartender to turn up the ballgame.

CHAPTER 14

DETECTIVE ROBINSON SORTED case files on his desk, which was so pristine that other cops sarcastically called him "Mr. Clean" on account of his obsession with keeping a neat desk. To him, it made sense to have a clean space to work.

Robinson was three weeks into the Katie Donnegan case. He opened up a package: McBain's cell records from Bell Atlantic. He riffled through them, noting that there were no calls on the night of the murder to a taxi company. But there were calls to numbers that interested him, including calls to a number registered to a South Boston flunky named Joseph Butters.

He decided to bring Butters downtown. That was what good cops did: They took statements and got the facts they needed. Then the next unhappy mess trundled down the assembly line. Robinson tapped a patrolman to pick up Butters, then drove him to the station. They walked him down to the interview room and let him molder for an hour.

Butters didn't have a care in the world. He just slumped in the chair loose as a bag of crushed chips, waiting for the blue boys to begin their tired routine.

Robinson strode in and put questions to him. He held paperwork in a thick file. Butters did the rope-a-dope routine, entirely unhelpful. He scratched his forehead and mumbled about not remembering anything special about that night.

"But you were out that night. At the Electric House, right?"

"Yeah."

"That's what you told us earlier."

"Well, that must be right then. That's when I saw the guy."

"You still driving a cab?"

"No."

"Your car, what do you—"

The door opened and Robinson looked up. It was Scott Magnus, his supervisor from the Homicide Unit. Robinson was irritated by the interruption, but he said nothing—it must be urgent. And Magnus had earned a reputation for a short fuse.

Magnus looked grim. "Step out for a moment, Detective."

"Sure." Robinson worked to keep his cool. Something was up. The situation pissed him off; it was unorthodox to have a fellow detective bust into the room during an interrogation.

They stepped out into the hall. Other cops hustled by. Magnus leaned toward him. "I'll handle it from this point. This guy Butters, we've been working him. A long time."

"What?"

"He's an asset. Relative to something we're working on long term. Can't have him in here."

"But I'd like to finish—"

"No." Magnus said.

Robinson felt his neck go red. "This is the Katie Donnegan murder."

"Appreciate your diligence, Detective. Really do."

"The phone records came—"

Magnus shook his head. "Give me the records and your file. I'll follow up."

Robinson saw a gelid look slide over Magnus' face. He knew this was turf not worth squabbling over. Still, this ploy by Magnus irked him.

When they got back in the room together, Robinson grabbed the phone records and shoved them at Magnus. Out of the corner of his eye, he saw a bewildered look crease Butters' face. Robinson shot him a look. Butters may be a valuable snitch, but this guy also had information on a murder. Yet Magnus was releasing him with no hesitation, ready to bury information that might spoil the golden boy.

Sometimes this job made him sick.

Robinson stalked out of the room, his face flushed with anger.

Magnus turned to Butters. "Get the fuck outta here."

Butters went to ask a question but the detective blew past him on his way out. He left the door wide open.

CHAPTER 15

BUTTERS WALKED DOWN the hallway. No one accosted him. No one asked him why he was leaving. Weird. He walked to the front door, out of the police station, and into the street. The hot night air blasted him with a chemical high.

He saw a car idling across the street. The driver gestured to him. His savior in a blue Monte Carlo—it was Riddick. He hung a beefy forearm out the window and gestured to the back seat. "Get in, we're going to a party."

Butters went to the passenger-side door. Butters knew better than to ask about what had just happened at the station. Someone cashed in some chips. It was a done deal, that was the important thing. Riddick's girlfriend, a skinny Puerto Rican-Irish half-breed named Marni, sat in front with a cigarette dangling out the window. She looked at him with her half-crazed smile. She was a glass freak. He never knew what Riddick saw in her. She was crazy, she must be giving him some voodoo sex, something he never had before.

Butters stepped inside the Monte Carlo, seats covered with fast food wrappers. He sat down and heard the crackle of a Styrofoam carton. This Monte was a rolling garbage dump.

They took D Street and drove to Burger King for burgers and fries. Then they drove toward the projects, pulled over on a side street, and stopped in front of a triple decker where a party was raging in the backyard. He could hear a steady rock beat thumping from the top floor.

"Whose party?"

"I dunno, someone at the bar wants us there." They walked around back into a wall of sound. A cookout was raging, with the scent of burnt hotdogs, suntan lotion, and the sickly sweet smell of ganja wafting on bass tones from the underworld.

Butters and Riddick maneuvered their way past the drunken crowd. Girls with boobs exploding out of halter tops, some oldsters playing cards at a picnic table, a few hard men in workout clothes drinking at a keg in the back. A guy brushed by and asked Butters if he wanted to buy some Quaaludes. Riddick was there before he could think to answer. "I'll knock your fuckin' roof in, Charlie, get outta here with that shit."

Butters saw Billy White from Old Colony, still with a limp from that stabbing incident at the ice rink last winter. They exchanged high fives and a bro hug.

"What the fuck," Billy said, a cigarette dangling from his deadman lips. "Do these kinds of injuries ever heal?"

Butters told him maybe he should see a doctor.

"I don't need no doctor," said Billy.

Riddick poured two plastic cups full of Narragansett. He stood with some of the guys near the keg and pounded back some brews.

A cute girl passed by in tight white shorts. He recognized her from high school. Someone joked about her doing the entire crew down at the beach last summer. The boys talked about her behind her back, made snide remarks. It was an old story. Yet when Butters heard it replayed again, her unchanging reputation, he felt a sadness creep over the waves of beer. It was a story he knew wasn't true. She was a good kid. But they trashed her reputation every time.

He thought of his girlfriend; she was mad at him again and they hadn't talked in a few days. He'd get something special for her birthday, maybe blotter acid. Or even some of that brown scag that was running through the projects this summer.

Riddick came back to the keg for a refill. "Hey Joey, hang tight," Riddick said. "They'll be wanting a word before long."

Butters looked at him steady. "Who?"

"You think favors grow on trees?"

"Okay." Another man gestured toward Riddick, who grabbed Butters by the elbow.

"In the basement. They want you now."

"Okay."

Butters was loaded from the beers he had dumped down his throat. He weaved over toward the cellar door. There was a hulking piece of meat with slits for eyes standing in front, his arms folded across a garage door chest.

"They told me to come down. I'm Joey Butters."

The guy nodded. "Come on in, kid." He leaned aside just enough for Butters to slide by.

Butters stepped into the cool air of the basement. He opened the door below and saw card tables, men gambling. A guy in a tan cap swore softly and slammed down his cards while the other men busted his ass for the crappy hand. More pounding rock music, cigarette smoke swirling in small clouds around the incandescent bulbs in the ceiling, half-eaten plates of ribs and empty cans of beer. No one was smoking weed down here though, the bosses didn't allow it.

Another guy gestured to him and he slipped into a little side room carved out of a crowded basement corner. It was substantial; plaster walls, no plywood. Two men walked out, almost knocking into him. Inside he saw four men sitting around a table. One of them was McBain, but he showed no sign of recognition. They were dressed in slacks and business shirts. One other guy at the table looked familiar. Not a guy he knew from the neighborhood, but he had the predatory face of someone you should listen to.

With a jolt, he recognized the face—the cop from Area D who had walked him out.

"Joey Butters, welcome. You get here okay?"

Butters nodded. He studied the man's face: washed-out features, like a figure in a wax museum. No emotion ran across his face. It was like watching a spot in a waterfall, tough to get a read.

"They treat you okay tonight?"

"Yeah."

The cop nodded. Then he got up and just walked out. McBain closed the door and the other men grew quiet.

"So, we appreciate what happened down there."

Butters said nothing.

"Still, you never should have been there. You gotta be smart."

The other two men, one with a bandana and dirty jeans, the other in painters' whites, got up and went to the other room. They came back with some small, knobby balls that looked like dirty white wax in their hands. He knew it was crack cocaine.

He smiled a bit. "Hey man, no thanks, I'm staying off that shit."

McBain just looked at him. The man in white took out a pipe and packed it full.

"Serious. I'm out." He hadn't smoked crack in two years and he was staying clean. This was why he never came out anymore.

"Hey. We're all friends. C'mon, you're one of the best. King of the projects." The men laughed around the table.

Butters was sweating now, heart rattling in the

cage. He had to get out of the basement. There was a palpable tension here, he felt it. They expected him to partake of the peace pipe. If he declined, maybe McBain would make it a problem.

They smoked and smoked and passed the pipe around. Again he declined. McBain and the cop, they expected his cooperation. They needed his friendship, needed him to be the slave. Any investigation by that damn cop Robinson could have been dangerous. Robinson was a thorough motherfucker, that was the word.

McBain told Butters several times he was the key to beating the case. All he had to do was tell the right story and put that guy Langford at the bar. But Langford was an innocent man.

What a thing to ask a man to do.

Butters glanced up and saw McBain's lean face looming through the smoky haze.

"You know what to do. These are our ways."

The men smoked, the music played, everyone was in a great mood. What was one hit? He should just get it over with. Butters took the pipe in his hands, an old friend who shared many memories. Then he inhaled.

The night went away as a million galaxies rose from the back of his eyeballs. He took another hit. His confidence was there, yes. He was once a king here. And he would be again.

PART 3

CHASING THE GHOST

Summer 2013

CHAPTER 16

Prison guard Vic Onager made the rounds on the cell block. He took a long look at the polite prisoner, Sam Langford. For over a dozen years, Langford had been his prisoner. Weird vibe with this guy. Prisoners ranged from disinterested to aggressive. With twenty years in the system, Onager had been cursed out by almost every animal on the farm, spit on, kicked in the leg, punched in the face, and one afternoon, shanked with a filed-down toothbrush.

But not Sam Langford. For the past few years, this goddamned killer had looked him in the eye and greeted him like a neighbor. A guy you see at the coffee shop. Made some small talk, but only when Onager started the conversation.

It pissed him off when Langford tried to masquerade as normal.

Onager walked back to the control desk and looked at the computer screen again. Maybe this time he would read a new tidbit somewhere.

Name: Langford, Samuel.

Known Aliases: None.

There were notes on tattoos (none) and gang affiliations (none). A CORI record showing a unique noninvolvement in the justice system, no prior cases. He had once seen a report with a thumbnail psychological sketch by a prison psychologist saying Langford had refused to accept blame for the crime he committed. But Langford had told the psychologist that he wanted to work. To learn to control the rage. "Because I will never admit guilt for something I didn't do. Because someday I plan on walking out of here."

Not every man in prison claimed to be innocent. Some boasted of their crimes, those who saw a criminal record as their only verifiable achievement in a wasted life. As the years slumped by, it became less important to deny the guilt. They just got on with passing the hours. But Langford had always insisted he was innocent. For years, he had turned down all offers of parole.

That was interesting.

Onager looked again at the notes. A note on a yard fight three years ago. Langford was defending himself against an aggressor. While he had done nothing wrong, he had apologized to the guards for being involved in a ruckus. He received no punishment.

Yes, it was very interesting with this guy. But Onager didn't believe the evidence. He took the lack of evidence as evidence. Evidence of something hidden. It was past time to put a stick between the bars and poke the bear a bit, see what the hell the deal was with Sam Langford.

Onager logged off the computer and strolled down the cell block.

CHAPTER 17

LANGFORD READ A book about the Civil War in his cell. Close to fifteen years in, you could get used to anything, he realized. Which was not the same thing as accepting it. As a kid he had played games like this—soldier, prisoner of war. How much shit can you take? Some say we all choose to be prisoners in some metaphysical way, but that could never compare to the real thing. When someone else did you royally, just screwed with you because they could.

Langford resisted the corrosive ways of prison at every turn. After the first year, he saw his midsection thickening up on the starchy meals. Macaroni and cheese, lots of bread, cheap cuts of meat. He responded by eating half of what they served. Let the state of Massachusetts fatten up other sheep for the system. He wanted no part of it. He read voraciously, exercised like a Spartan, volunteered in the library—the necessary diversions of a life behind bars and concrete. Langford looked for ways to fill his days, when each day looked and smelled like every other day on the assembly line.

For a long time he played a game in his mind. He had grown up in a row house near Boston harbor. Nothing special, but a good solid home, woodwork around the doorways, shingled exterior painted something his father always called Colonial red. His father hoed the ground on the west side—tomatoes, potatoes, and zucchini erupted in late summer. Each morning he dreamed of walking through the old house, yelling something to his mother, eating breakfast in the nook near the window overlooking the harbor while his dad toiled below in the yard. Some days he dreamed of his return to Southie, when he would paint the rooms a certain color, move furniture around, dig up the vegetables.

But as the years slid by, he started thinking of the old house less and less. And as time slipped further along, he stopped thinking of it at all. His mom died and only his father and sister remained. His old cellmate once warned him about dreaming about the past or the future. Dreams weren't about getting out. They were about getting by.

He heard a rattling in the air ducts as the ventilation switched on. He learned over time just how much sheer joy came from his sense of smell. The nose was the gateway where the most pernicious temptations entered. Good food, flowers, fresh air, a woman's skin, all were a distant memory. When spring came, his body was fit for bursting as some primordial rhythm slipped into gear. The first day in May last year, he walked out to the yard and felt tears roll down his face, that was how sweet the air smelled. He had looked away from the others to hide his reaction. Then he noticed one or two other men doing the same thing, hunched over to hide the sudden show of emotion, the loss of control. When the breeze blew in his face again, he came to the end of caring and just stood there, feeling the breeze rush over his forehead and past his ears, his sinews writhing.

"Sam, how goes it?"

His reverie interrupted, Sam put the book down. A guard, Onager was the name, was peering into the small, barred window in the door.

"Living day by day. Day by day."

Onager nodded, looked down the hallway, and then back in at Langford. "The innocent man," said Onager.

Sam hesitated and did not respond at first.

"Oh, come on! Everyone knows you've been moping around here for years claiming you didn't kill that girl. Ain't that right, Sam? You're innocent. Despite your day in court where twelve jurors said you did. You raped and killed that girl." Onager's face loomed in the narrow window.

Langford never discussed his case out in the open. No prisoner did. Guards hated those stories. They did not appreciate the implication that maybe some of their security work involved guarding innocent people. That kind of thinking could corrode the mind.

"I did nothing to that girl. I swear to God."

"Trial by water, Sammy boy. We'll see."

Langford didn't know what Onager was talking about. But he didn't like the tone.

From down the row, Langford heard someone call Onager a fatfuck hack. It was one of the Collier brothers, whose warped DNA had ruined generations of the family. Onager stepped back and looked down the hallway. Langford delved back into his book. But Onager soon turned back.

"You a southpaw?"

Langford looked up again. But then a call came in from the security desk.

Onager took the call and turned to Langford. "Lucky for you. A visitor."

Langford got up. Onager and another guard cuffed him and walked him down the block to the visiting rooms. Onager walked Langford toward a room and uncuffed him.

Langford looked inside the room and saw a man with dark hair and a corded neck dressed in an expensive-looking dark jacket—his investigator Ray Infantino was sitting at the table.

Ray stood up and shook hands with Langford. Onager stared at them both. Ray turned and glanced at Onager as he lingered at the door. He shook his head as if pondering something beyond the understanding of the human race.

Ray and Langford watched Onager as he walked away.

"What's up with that dude?" Ray asked.

"Not sure. Anyway, let's forget about him—I am surprised to see you."

Ray settled in and discussed the investigation as Langford stretched his legs.

"I met with Butters," Ray said. "We have an angle with him. He was guarded at first, told me almost nothing. Poor memory, meds, the usual bullshit. So we went into what he was doing walking that night. I brought up the orange taxi, the one seen by the old lady, Mrs. Farrell. He did not handle that very well. Looked like he saw a ghost."

"How do you mean?"

"Not sure yet, but there might be something—a witness, old records—that links Butters to the taxi company."

"So it's something we can use?"

"Yes, it is. I think Butters probably picked up Katie that night."

They needed Butters to talk. Most Americans held a deep belief that rugged individualism should be honored, that there was a right to be left alone. But Butters was in the crosshairs now. The orange cab was a hot lead, and they could not leave him alone.

"So what's next?" Langford asked.

"Keep pulling the threads until the case breaks open. I need to go see the victim's family."

CHAPTER 18

RAY DROVE SOUTH on the highway to Rhode Island, taking the Sakonnet River Bridge out to a ridge running alongside the river. Although Rhode Island is the smallest state in the country, the shoreline of Narragansett Bay runs for hundreds of miles, glaciers having pulled the land like taffy into haphazard shapes. He pulled over on a dead-end road. Behind a long stretch of beach grass he could hear the soft lapping of ocean waves. He looked over at a small blue cottage with a cedar fence silvered by the salt air and waited.

Meeting with families of crime victims was tough work. Some families refused to talk, a decision reflecting rage, grief, or some other point on a spectrum of shattering loss. He respected that limit when people asked to be left alone. Others understood the reason behind his visit—a criminal case in which the facts were in dispute, where a witness held up by a prosecutor as a paragon of truth-telling had buried the shabby details of his life. Others spoke out of a sense of avoiding entanglement in a case where they would need to testify. Some seemed almost eager to talk, just to weave some threads back into an outline of the face of a lost son or daughter.

The grace they displayed often amazed him. The murder of a loved one cratered the joy of a family; it was almost beyond imagination. But these interviews were necessary, for another life was in the balance. When someone lost their freedom, that was justice for an act of violence. But at times they took freedom from the wrong person. And while prison lacked the finality of the grave, it was tinged with a little death of its own. The death of hope, of respect, of all the small, pleasant rituals of life outside a cage.

Ray took a deep breath and walked up a white pathway of crushed shells. He was superstitious about these things so he had gotten up early and taken a moment to choose the right clothes. He wore his best navy blue shirt with a beige jacket, set off with a blue-and-white Versace tie that cost a small fortune and a pair of brown, American-made wingtip shoes. Given who he was going to see, it was a day to dress up, show respect. It was the right look. He needed every advantage.

The door opened before he could knock. A woman with a lined face and sharp gaze appearing to be in her gray fifties stood in the doorway. "Can I help you?"

"Good morning, Mrs. Donnegan. I'm Ray

Infantino, working on an appeal on an old criminal case. Your daughter's case." He trailed off and let her absorb it. She gazed at him. "There are some questions about one of the witnesses."

"Are you a police officer?"

"No. I'm a private investigator. Sam Langford is my client."

A spasm of pain crossed her face. "Is he getting out?"

"Well, there are some things that came up that raise some questions about whether he is the right guy. I can explain if you have a moment."

He half-expected the door to swing shut in his face. But Mrs. Donnegan just opened up the door and let him inside. She invited him to sit down in a living room decorated in muted whites. There were maritime knick-knacks all over. A piece of driftwood hung on the wall. The coffee table was a wood lobster trap, the kind they stopped making decades ago.

"There are some questions about the ID made by one of the witnesses, Mrs. Donnegan. He seems to have been a police informant. He worked with them on other cases."

"Please, call me Mary Ann." She sat down across from him. "I remember one man. Not his name, but that day he got called as a witness. Not a likable guy. None of them seemed like upstanding people, you know? It kind of surprised me. But what does this have to do with this case now?"

"My question was about your daughter's

knowledge of a guy named Joseph Butters. He testified in the case."

"Yes, that's the name. Butters, I remember that."

"Butters testified at trial that he saw Sam Langford with Katie outside the bar that night."

"I always wondered about him."

"Why?"

"Mother's intuition. I don't know." Mary Ann shook her head. "He just seemed off."

"Do you think she knew Butters before that night?"

"Oh God, no. She knew none of these people. We're from Rhode Island. She had no connection to Boston before. It was a new thing. All of them were strangers."

"Did she socialize in Boston at all? Maybe have friends there?"

"No. She was a beach kid. That weekend was her first time going to the city alone. She really didn't like big cities."

"So Joe Butters was not a name you were familiar with."

"No."

"Do you happen to have her old phone, by any chance?"

"I do. They gave it to me at the morgue. I went to identify the body, and they gave me her belongings. It was in her purse."

This interested him. "The police never asked for the phone?"

"No. I never thought it was important."

"Would you mind if I looked at it?"

Mary Ann got up and went into a back room. Ray looked around the living room again. There were family photos on a wall next to an oak bookcase. The family frozen in time—the sepia years of the 1950s, showing well-dressed grandparents holding a baby; a washed-out Polaroid from the 1970s; more recent photographs with sharp colors. Katie, he could see her in the new ones, a pretty blonde with fair skin and a smile that lit the day. Ray felt a current of sadness roll through him as he looked at her. The daughter every father would be proud to call his own. And the thing that happened to her that no one in those photos would ever forget. Nothing could change that fact that she was gone. You accepted things as they barreled beneath you, rode the waves, or you went under.

He heard Mary Ann coming back in the room and he brushed his forehead. It felt like his eyeballs were peeling off. Ridiculous; he was getting to be like an old lady, weeping on the job after looking at some old photos. He looked away. Mary Ann paused and looked into his face, seeming to recognize something there.

"I'm sorry. I didn't mean to pry," he said.

"It's alright. She had a smile that could do that." She touched his arm and sat down with a sigh. "I still break into tears all the time. It's been so many years now. Yet I still talk to her like she can hear me."

"Yes. I'm sorry for it."

"You're not supposed to bury your children. You never deal with it. Not really."

Mary Ann handed him the phone and, to his surprise, the power cord. The phone was huge by comparison to modern cell phones, a heavy gray brick.

"If you think it will help, you can turn it on, take a look. Should we bring this to the police?"

"You could. I'm not sure what that would do, though. In their mind, this case is over."

"Yes, that's true."

He plugged in the phone and waited while it powered up. After a minute or two the screen glowed and Ray scrolled down a log of past phone calls. The final call was made at 1:03 a.m. with the Boston 617 area code.

"Do you know this number?"

"No."

"Are you sure your daughter didn't have any friends in Boston?"

"Not that I know of. What do you think she was doing?"

"Someone used her phone to make a call." He jotted down the number in his notes. "I appreciate your time, thank you again." Ray said.

Mary Ann walked him out to the car. He drove for a while and then pulled over to a cafe. He got coffee and logged into a database to reverse the phone number. The number came back to a taxi company,

Athens Taxi. He dialed the number himself and confirmed it was inactive. Maybe Katie had called a cab company herself? Did the cops run down the cabbie who drove to the bar? Or check for links to Butters working as a driver? An old murder case was like a game where dead men switched out their bones.

Next he checked on the history of Athens Taxi. The cab company was owned by a Greek immigrant who had died in the mid-1990s. He sold the company, and the taxi medallions were purchased by bigger firms like Checker Cab, Charles River, and Metro Taxi. Every single photo he found of Athens taxis showed they sported bright orange paint.

CHAPTER 19

IT WAS DARK by the time he reached downtown Boston. He planned to meet Jose Marquez at The Orleans Club in the South End, where some of the boys were shooting pool and making tortuous conversation with women well outside their age range. Marquez was his oldest friend. They went back together to high school, a footballer heavier by thirty pounds now and with heavy-lidded eyes that made him look like an amorous lizard.

"Hey, look who's here," said Marquez. "The private dick. Watch yourselves, ladies, this guy is the danger man." Ray pulled down a cue stick and jumped in a game. Marquez took a sip of a seasonal ale from a North Shore brewery. "You getting your usual highball, miss?" he asked Ray.

"Vodka tonic."

"I read this article today—if you drink vodka late at night, it interferes with your sleep patterns."

"Goddamn scientists. They're not leaving us anything."

Marquez snorted in the background as Ray promptly sank an eight ball.

"Rack 'em, baby."

"I love when you talk dirty," Marquez said.

"I love taking your money."

The bartender sent over some pizzas and drinks and Ray settled into a spot along the wall, waiting for the game to end. He slipped into the barroom banter, but the visit with the dead girl's mother weighed on his mind. He grew quiet.

Eventually the verbal carom shots and the billiards table worked their magic. The adrenaline coursed in his veins. By midnight, he shed the grip of the day. He wanted to enjoy the night out with the lads. But it occurred to him this was a night just like another night so many years ago, when Sam Langford walked by a different bar, filled with different people, and saw it all end for him, at least in the way he once knew.

He took a sip of his drink. A group of men in white dress shirts—soft, pudgy types in their twenties, probably stock brokers or bankers—were playing at the next pool table. They were getting rambunctious. They were ordering top-shelf whiskies and bourbons in loud voices, showing off the tastes of the well-to-do. Beacon Hill boys or waterfront up-and-comers.

Ray was mauling Marquez again. He stepped to

the table to bury an eight ball for the win when he felt a sharp jab in the ribs. He turned and saw one of the billowy white shirts mumble an apology and move away, his back already turned. Ray said nothing. He let his gaze linger for a few seconds longer than polite company would condone and turned back to the table. Marquez was observing him.

"You good?"

"Fine."

"Looked like you were gonna do dental surgery on a banker."

Ray shook his head. "No. He is a dick. But no, my barroom brawl days are behind me." A few minutes later, a waitress returned with several more shots for the other group. One of the men, tall with a pot belly and shaggy hair styled such that he looked a man-sized rodent, said something in an undertone. The waitress stiffened, buried her head, and went back to putting drinks down on a table.

"I'm sorry, I thought you ordered Bushmills. I'll get you the reserve again."

"Keep them coming, honey," the tall man said. As the waitress walked away, the guy said to her back, "Fuck that up again, I'll roger your holes out with this cue."

The table burst out laughing. The waitress didn't seem to hear the remark. Ray and Marquez did. Marquez looked over and shook his head, but Ray was already moving toward the man. He got up close and smiled. "You say that again to her and that cue is likely to disappear up your ass."

The pool table went silent. Ray lifted his pool cue in a mock toast. Then he leaned down to resume the game, aimed, and buried the shot.

The tall rodent man stepped toward him. Ray could tell the guy's confidence was growing as he evaluated his height advantage in the sunlight of bourbon fumes. "Mind your business, friend."

"We are," Ray said. He felt Marquez coming up behind him as the other men caught a sniff of something happening. "We know her. And you will tip her $200 tonight for that comment."

The big guy walked straight up to him and looked down with a little smile playing across his face. Ray could smell waves of foul-smelling liquor wafting from the man's skin. It was always like this with drunks, they had no sense of hygiene. Then the guy snarled and fired off a punch, a slow and lazy thing. Ray slipped it easily and then came twisting out of a crouch with a left hook, drilling the man in the ribs, then coming upstairs with a second punch to the jaw, then a straight right to clean up whatever was left still standing. The big man went sprawling into the pool table and sent the brightly colored balls rolling across the table.

Ray didn't wait. His hands twitched with a surplus of adrenaline. A feeling of pure, elemental rage coursed through him. He wanted to humiliate this arrogant shit-bum. He stepped to the table, bent his leg back, and kicked the man as hard as he could in the backside, sending him to the ground. Marquez was moving past him now and launching punches randomly into any bankers' faces and stomachs he could reach. Expensive whiskey spilled to the floor. Someone was yelling. Ray's opponent made panting sounds as he lurched to his hands and knees half-heartedly. The big man looked around at the spilled drinks and his cowed friends in baggy white dress shirts, who were hanging back with looks of uncertainty on their faces. Brawls during pool games were seen on cable TV, not in real life. He raised his hands and signaled he wanted nothing more.

Ray's neck felt like it was burning and his sense of control was ebbing. He stepped toward the man, who shrank back with hands raised. Then hands came down on him from behind. He reared back until he heard the voices of his friends. "Enough, Ray, easy man. This thing's over." Even while some part of him knew his response was terribly out of proportion with what had transpired, he still wanted to blast this guy through the floorboards. Deliver a lesson worth remembering.

His friends were whispering to him closeup and he felt his anger pass away on the words like a puff of black smoke. He watched it drift out of his head and regained control of his breathing. He needed to let this go, it was not worth it. They were in the pub and shooting pool and many people he knew were looking at him with a mixture of joy, respect, and disgust, sometimes all of them at once.

The waitress came back to the table and moved around the broken man like he was just another piece of furniture. Just trying to do her job. She nodded to Ray with a look of concern on her face, which struck him as odd. "I've seen you here before but you should leave here tonight. Take a break."

Maybe she pitied him. He nodded. It seemed like a good idea.

"I'll call you later," Marquez said.

Ray walked out of the bar while Marquez tended to the fallen.

CHAPTER 20

THE NEXT MORNING Ray took a call from Marquez and made plans to meet at The Roxbury Diner. He dressed in chinos and boots and a dark silk shirt and took a walk through the quiet side streets to Shawmut. It was a beautiful morning in the city. He got to the diner and saw Marquez had commandeered a table near a window. Ray looked over at a plate of eggs and home fries being served to the table next door. "Eat like that, you come out a little older than when you got here," Ray said.

"Yeah, they kinda overdo it with home fries here. But I love this joint."

"Good night of pool."

"Yes." Marquez looked at him for a minute and frowned. "What was happening with you last night? You never used to react like that. That guy saw his life pass before his eyes. You should have seen your face. You were gonna kill him. I could see it in your eyes."

"It was a bit too much."

"Ray, please. The guy's six feet plus and you're tearing into this guy like he's a scarecrow. I've never seen you like this."

"Right."

"You should talk about it."

Ray laughed. "What do you mean, see a psychologist?"

"This is not the 1950s, buddy. People can help you control your anger. You got too much to lose."

He thought about it. Marquez was right, but he still struggled with the concept. Too many people were dumping their anguish, and he just preferred to deal with it a different way.

"Why is everyone so afraid of one guy getting pissed off once in a while?"

Marquez just shook his head. "That was not just anger last night. Way past that. You went a ways down the highway."

Ray said nothing.

"Talk to someone. You should consider it. Even mob bosses see shrinks now."

"That was television, brother."

"Life imitates art. Try it. You can't keep going this way."

A waitress came by to pour them coffee. Ray shook a sugar packet and stirred his coffee.

"So what's going on? Something at work?"

"Just the usual. Innocent people getting fucked."

"How is the lady in California?"

"It's probably over with Dominique."

Marquez took that in and nodded. "Sorry to hear that. What happened?"

"The distance is too much," Ray said. "And some things happened where she thinks something happened with a woman when nothing did. But there is mistrust."

"We're worried about you. You're not around much these days."

"It's been busy. Every year, I'm taking on a dozen cases with innocent men in prison. I'm supposed to get them out. There is pressure. The cases consume you."

"They're all innocent in there, right?" Marquez joked.

"This guy actually is." Ray changed the topic. "Look, I think last night was bad, don't get me wrong. I'm working on it."

"OK. We watching the football game Saturday?"

"Yeah, we'll hammer the Dolphins. They don't show up north of Miami."

A waitress came by and Ray ordered an omelet with Portuguese sausage and peppers. Marquez ordered the Kitchen Sink, which included almost every item on the menu; eggs, bacon, waffles, pancakes, and a slice of pie.

"You will jam those arteries up tight before noontime."

Marquez shrugged. "So this case, is that the murder at the bar, the Electric House?"

"That's the one."

"You worry about working on those things?"

"I don't think about it too much."

"You're in the business of, you know, kinda pissing people off. The right people. But still."

"These cases grab you. What can I say? I talked to the mother of the victim yesterday in that case..." Ray trailed off. "The DA who prosecuted Langford is now a judge. The police reports we have don't make sense. And the reports we need are missing. If you exonerate one guy, it means someone else did the crime. So there is a lot of unhappiness rippling out to the edge." He sipped his coffee and pointed a finger at the ceiling. "I might just become a painter. I told you that before."

"Housepainter is more like it," Marquez laughed. "I've seen some of your crazy shit. But you had some artistic skill."

"I still have it."

"Ahh, you're not quitting the detective gig anytime soon. You love it too much." Marquez grew serious. "Listen man, we got your back. Think about what I said. If you need anything, don't forget to ask."

Ray nodded. "Thanks."

The waitress came by with their breakfasts and the table got quiet as the men went to work on the eggs. They talked more about football and Ray relaxed. Then he checked his watch.

"I gotta run, I have to go see another guy in Southie, an old snitch for the BPD. More fun and games."

They finished breakfast and parted ways. Ray made his way over to the garage and pulled out the Shelby. Time to see Davin Price. He took Congress Street into the Seaport District and pulled up behind a new apartment complex near the hotels.

Price had gone upscale, fleeing the squalor of his housing project youth. The security in the lobby was lame and Ray was walking down the eighth-floor hallway within minutes. He knocked and waited. Then a lean face with shoulder-length hair peered out a crack in the door. The face wore a look of concern.

"Mr. Price, I'm looking into an old case. You have a moment?"

"Huh? How did you get in?"

"Security was not too secure."

"Yeah, tell me about it."

"Just making a courtesy call before this case gets going. I'm not a cop."

"Well, okay. What's your name again?"

"Ray Infantino."

"What's this about?"

"Sam Langford."

"Who?"

"Murder case from a few years ago. Girl at the Electric House."

"Oh. I remember that guy. Long time ago."

"Just take a minute."

He saw Davin hesitate and look down at the floor. "Sorry pal, I don't want to get involved in someone else's shit." There was a high-pitched tone to his voice now.

"Might save everyone a hassle down the road."

"How?"

"This thing is still alive. There are going to be hearings, new trial, appeals. The beautiful thing about these cases is they never end. Keep a lot of people employed."

Price hesitated, muttered something about being sorry, and then closed the door. Ray raised his voice. "Please, Davin, just a minute. Is something wrong?" No answer. "I'll leave a number here if you change your mind." Ray slid a business card along the door-jamb, and headed out to the street.

When he got outside, he looked up at the side of the building. He could see the silhouette of a head peering from behind the curtains. A fitting image for a snake. Ray stood on the sidewalk and waved as he snapped a picture of the head-shaped shadow behind the curtain. The shadow disappeared. He laughed and then headed toward downtown, letting Price stew for a while in his guilty memories. He would see Price again in due time.

CHAPTER 21

Ray waved to his neighbors as he pulled into his garage in the South End. He got to his building and walked to the living room, where huge potted palms fingered the windowsills. He sat down and thought for a moment. The conversation at breakfast reminded him it was time he called Dominique.

"How is your day going?" he asked.

"Good." There was a long silence from her. It had gone like this the last few calls. She was off somewhere else, he could sense it. Normally, the two of them never groped for words, but now there was an awkwardness to their conversations.

"What's happening with the cases?" she asked.

"Not much."

"Is she still working for you?"

He knew who she was without a first name. "Yes, Tania works here."

"How long are you going to let her go at this?"

Ray said nothing. She had been telling him for a year

about her misgivings. "It's irresponsible to send her out there."

"She's ready. She's strong. She wants to work—"

"It's too early. It's too close to things she dealt with in her own life."

"She is an adult, Dominique. She's good at this kind of work. People open up to her. You can't stop her."

Dominique's voice took a cool turn. "You could. She works for you. Let her work on something else."

"It's her choice to work. I'll send her where I think she can be effective."

"Well, in this case, freedom to choose is bullshit. She's misguided."

Ray felt a surge of frustration. "You're wrong."

It had gone like this since Tania left San Francisco after enduring a long rehabilitation. At first, Tania had completely iced him. She barely spoke a word in those early weeks, blaming him for what happened in the end: Members from the Black Fist triad tracked her and her partner Moon to an apartment, resulting in a shooting that left Moon dead and Tania badly injured.

He visited her at the hospital, stopping by to check on her every few weeks. She never told him to stop visiting. Eventually, she seemed to come to some understanding that Moon's death was not his fault. There was no heated discussion. She just started talking one day and a little more the next until they were in full conversation.

She took a full year to return to some semblance of her former self. A petite woman, she had lost twenty pounds after the shooting. But she regained her strength in fierce bursts, a feat of willpower, pushing her body up like a rose through the cracks toward the light. Maybe too hard, he first thought. A slow metamorphosis took place. First she grew her hair out and wore it down to her shoulders, pulled back to show her arresting features. She emerged as if from a long journey underground, spare and harder than before.

The criminal trial for one of the triad shooters who had survived dragged on through the summer. Both Ray and Tania testified. The feds were building a RICO case against Victoria Chang after Ray's investigation exposed the role of her attorney, Lucas Michaels, in shielding her empire at every turn in a decades-long scheme of tax evasion, money laundering, and murder of rival gangsters.

Then, after that long process was over, Tania had approached Ray with a strange request: She wanted to work as a private detective.

At first, he refused to consider it. They had spent months planning to keep her off the radar of the gang. But she persisted, telling him a life on the run was no life at all. And he better than anyone should know that—she reminded him he had told her this when he'd found her.

Ray took her on. He felt he owed her that at least. First working the databases in the safety of the office, background and asset work. She showed a smart, relentless mind. But she was interested in other difficult aspects of the work, interviewing witnesses and suspects, and in particular, a missing persons case. The location was San Diego. The missing girl, eighteen, had run off with an older man she met on the internet. He led a clannish religious group that in another era would have had neon lights flashing the word "revival meeting" in the desert night. Now they had a website and recruited new members by selling podcast subscriptions on how to liberate your mind, sue your parents, and donate money to the cause. Tania went back to California and delved into the case with zeal.

Since Tania's reemergence, Dominique had, strangely to Ray's mind, assumed a motherly stance toward her, as if she had adopted her and was now in charge of a young, wayward child. Tania was an adult woman. What Ray saw as growing confidence, Dominique saw as an obsession for danger. Ray pointed out that nothing she did now was as dangerous as her previous work as a prostitute.

Dominique had gotten to the point. "You still seem to have more than a professional interest in her. I think it's gone that far."

"Ahh, so that is where we are. Given she's not within a thousand miles of me, I don't see anything happening."

"That's not how I see it."

Silence.

"Have you slept with her?"

"Never. That's not what happened."

This angered him; it was baseless. He started to fashion a sarcastic barb, but stopped when he heard the pain in her silence. He listened to her breathing at the end of the line. She was a million miles away from him now.

"I gotta go," she said. "I don't know what else to say to you right now."

"The answer is no."

"It's okay, Ray. Maybe our time has come and gone."

Ray got up and looked out the window, thinking back to the night just before Tania began working for him. He had unexpectedly run into Tania at a restaurant in Marin a year out from her recovery. He caught sight of a woman at the bar, thick dark hair and an earthy laugh. The woman turned around, and it was her. The sight shocked him; he glimpsed Tania as she once was, or had been described to him, he wasn't sure of the line anymore. She glowed with the aura of someone free of the past. Some people spend a life trying to accomplish that feat, and yet she seemed to move to the open road ahead.

He stopped for a drink with her. After her friends left, they sat at the bar and talked openly about that horrific day on Telegraph Hill—the triad gang members invading the house, Tania injured, Moon bleeding out, Ray wallowing in ineffectual rage. They relived the high-speed roar of the flight from the Marin Hills to hiding out while triad soldiers on a kill mission closed in on Telegraph Hill.

They drove back to his home and, once there, just held each other. There was no sex. There was a place beyond the base physical needs people exploited a million times every day. He knew at that moment that human touch was the first path, would be the final path through dust and whatever lay beyond. The next morning they spoke, laughing over breakfast, and the thing, while not forgotten, would not lead to anything further. And they were satisfied with that.

Ray told Dominique later about what had happened. They were discussing long-term plans and considering a move to the coast. So he told her everything. Dominique had absorbed it calmly enough; nothing had happened, after all. But the event eroded trust and the ghost of suspicion roamed. The event involved Ray and Tania, but not Dominique, and that broke their bond. He struggled to understand how two people who once spoke so easily together could now stumble around a conversation. But it was clear that they were coming to an end.

It was a Sunday evening when they last spoke together in person. As they spoke together across a table, they heard an echo of laughter from a distant playground as the sun slashed down on people walking the street, people heading to a destination where someone loved them, or didn't love them. A place where someone was alone and shadows loomed across the floor as everything moved to rest.

Dominique decided she was staying in California. Ray had a moment where he thought he would protest, but his vigor for battle was spent. They left each other in peace, but that didn't make the pain any less. He had failed her, failed to meet that most basic of human needs: to feel loved.

CHAPTER 22

LATE IN THE evening, Langford was reading his book on Civil War history when two shapes appeared at the window of his cell. The door opened. Two guards stepped in. One of them was Onager.

"You have a visitor," he said.

Langford hesitated. It was late for visitors; even his legal team rarely visited this late at night. Maybe Ray Infantino had come down. He seemed like the type to work late.

"Langford, move it."

Langford got up and walked down the hallway toward the interview rooms. The prison was still. He heard the door behind him open and clang shut. The guards led him to the foyer.

The interview rooms were empty. There were no lawyers waiting, no one at all. The white plastic chairs, the desk, no paperwork, nothing. He looked around. A chill ran up his neck. Onager stood silently behind him. Then another door clanged open down the hall. A shadow moved along the wall.

Someone was coming.

The guard removed his shackles. He heard Onager laugh.

"Come on, Sammy boy, my money's on you. No shanks, just bare knuckles."

Now he understood. Gladiator matches. He looked up as the shadow grew into a man-shape. A young kid with dark, sinewy arms and Mexican gang tattoos running down his neck. His eyes were hard, unfeeling, and his fists were ready to fly.

Langford yelled, "No," but the kid was already on him.

Langford went down under the bullrush, but avoided any blows to his face. They rolled around on the cement. Langford staggered up, but an elbow caught him on the side of the head. Langford set his feet and threw a right cross that cracked off the Mexican's skull. That backed him up for a moment. There was a lull as the men circled each other.

Langford heard Onager's voice and several others urging the fighters, voices eager yet restrained at the same time. The guards were placing bets on the blood flow.

Langford fired a few jabs to keep the Mexican off him. The Mexican circled him and threw several haymakers, grunting with venomous intent. Langford blocked the punches, but one caught him below the left eye. He recoiled, and the Mexican blasted him with a flurry of punches. Langford felt his desperation growing. The Mexican was younger and would eventually wear him down.

Langford knew he had to end it soon. Feinting, Langford lunged and landed a right uppercut into the man's gut. The man grunted and staggered, and Langford was on him, burying him with sheer bulk. The men sprawled on the cement, both breathing heavily now. Langford hammered a fist on the man's cheek, smashing and smashing to slow him down. He saw blood running from the man's eyes. There was a pause as both men gasped for oxygen. Their movements slowed. They moved like an odd, doubled-backed animal, all whipping legs and grunts. Finally Langford's greater size seemed to weigh on the younger man. Both men stopped struggling. "This is what they want," Langford whispered. "Let it go." The younger man seemed to go slack.

He heard Onager yell. "Break it up, boys!" Hands pulled Langford to his feet. He held tight to his opponent, fearing a cheap shot. But the guards dragged the Mexican away from him and across the floor.

Onager's glowing face appeared above him. "Round one! 10 - 9 for Canelo." He looked around with a satisfied smile. "Clear out now." Onager flung a towel at Langford's feet. "Wipe up the damn floor, Langford. I don't want to see your snot here in the morning."

Langford gulped deep breaths of air to steady himself. His breathing was slowly returning to normal.

Then he got on his hands and knees and scrubbed the floor. He grimaced as a pain shot through his ribs.

When he was finished, Onager and another guard led Langford back to his cell. They led the Mexican back down the hallway. The rest of the guards faded into the yard.

Langford staggered into his cell and washed the blood off his face. Round two was coming soon. He wondered how many rounds he could go. How long could he hope to keep the young gangbanger off him?

Then he crawled into his bed to sleep off the pain.

CHAPTER 23

RAY WAS READING through some police reports when a call came in. "This call is from a correctional facility and may be monitored and recorded." It was Sam Langford. He accepted the call and listened as Langford described the fight staged by the guards the night before. He could tell that the incident shook up Langford. Ray told him he would drive there within an hour.

A second call came in, this one from Tania. Things had stalled in California and an incident the night before had spooked her: She thought a car had followed her back to her apartment. Ray thought the time was ripe to pull her out of San Diego. He told her to drive straight to the airport and come back to Boston.

He dressed in a suit and drove to the prison in the midmorning sun. Off to the left, Gillette Stadium, home of the New England Patriots, loomed over the roadway. He turned into the back roads that led to a clearing in the woods where the massive, gray-walled prison took its turn dominating the landscape. He went through security, got patted down, and headed through the yard out to the attorney meeting rooms. Ray waited. Then he heard chains shaking and saw the guard come from the cells with his client.

Langford was in considerable pain. There was a fresh cut below his eye, his shoulders slumped, and he looked bent as an old piece of driftwood. He slumped into the chair and looked at the floor. The guard left them alone. Ray closed the door behind him.

"What happened?"

"Guy came at me. Gladiator fights. Just a bullshit thing they do in here," he said, gesturing to the cut. "I'm worried about this one guard. He has it in for me."

"Who?"

"You remember the guard you saw last time? Name is Onager, something like that. He wants to fuck with me. With anyone. Even the other guards tell me he's an asshole. He set this thing up. And it's going to happen again until one of us gets killed. They even did a cell check, and he wrote me up on some bullshit." Langford sagged and put his forehead to his hand.

Ray leaned toward him. "Don't let this piece of shit take you down."

"I'm fighting it. I appealed the writeup. They'll set a hearing. No one ever wins in those things. But I'll tell them about the fights." He looked down. "It is hard taking this shit from someone who thinks they know you. Thinks you're guilty. And that gives them a right to pull at you until you unravel. Christ."

Ray reached out and touched Langford's shoulder. All the starch had run out of him. Ray was worried. He had never seen the man so down.

"We will make some calls to the legal department. This is going to stop."

"Outside these walls, that fucking guy wouldn't have the balls to look me straight in the eye. In here, he's like a king." They sat for a while. Langford stewed but finally came around. "Well, let's talk about the case. Anything happening?"

Ray briefed him on the progress so far with Katie's mother in Rhode Island and Price.

The cell phone information intrigued Langford. "What makes guys like Butters and Price get up and lie like that?" Langford asked. "How do you do that to someone? Some guy you don't even know?"

"That's what makes it easy. They don't know you."

"Before I got here, I never realized this world existed—prison gangs, snitches."

"Most people don't. Most people would recoil if you told them the government paid a witness a thousand dollars to testify. But the government can wipe ten years off the sentence of a snitch. What is the value in a year of freedom?"

They talked over their next moves and who they wanted to see. Langford seemed revived once they finished work for the day. They stood, the plastic chairs scraping on the floor. Ray embraced him and patted his shoulders.

"I appreciate you coming on short notice," Langford said, gripping his hand. "Good to get some conversation each day. Thank you, Ray."

"Keep an eye on the finish line. That's what will get you there."

"I know." He scratched his leg beneath the cheap, threadbare, orange prison garb stained with food and other gunk. "Toughest thing is knowing you got your family out there waiting."

"They come to see you this week?"

"My sister will. She believed none of it, thank God. She comes on weekends." Langford got quiet then. "Last time she came, I noticed how much older she looks. Your entire family gets sentenced. They do the time you do. In a different way, maybe, but it's hard on them. It's always later than you think." Langford looked down, his face wet. "But no sob stories from me. We gotta work on me getting out of here. My sister tells me stories about our old neighborhood, the little restaurants that open, new places that spring up. I like to hear it all."

"Good. Where do you want to go when you get out of here?"

"First day, I'll go to this place called The Palms. We always loved it. Get a steak and some ice cream," he said with a laugh. "After that, there is so much waiting for me. It will be a crazy thing to see." He trailed off. "If I stay alive long enough to see it."

"Eye on the prize," Ray said. He nodded through the plexiglass window toward the guard. "Never let them see you down."

If Langford heard him, he gave no sign. He stared out the window. The guard was standing at the door. He watched as Langford took the long, clanking walk back to the cells.

A sick feeling rose in Ray's belly. The dice roll of a prison fight. Two men fighting in an isolated concrete hallway, desperate breaths of air, grinning guards laying down their bets. Things were swirling around this case. And no matter what he did outside, the fact was that Langford was feeling the blowback behind these walls.

They were running out of time.

CHAPTER 24

ON THE WAY back from the prison, Ray met with some clients downtown and then headed back to the office. Tania was flying from San Diego and expected to be back by nightfall. Summer was stretching toward autumn as a low evening sun set. The breeze was tipped with a hint of crisp umber leaves. He took Storrow Drive past a row of Back Bay brownstones, silent sentinels lining the riverbank. A glorious afternoon on the Charles, the blue water dotted with white sails, willow trees shimmying in the breeze. Runners dotted the crumbling trails, while a few scantily clad girls sunned themselves on the river bank and drew an inordinate amount of attention.

He got back to the office, put some Junior Kimbrough on the sound system, and buried himself in work. It was past seven when the doorbell rang and Tania came in, brushing off the dust of travel, trailing bags and electronics. After a quick embrace, they went out back to the patio. He opened a bottle of wine and poured her a glass. She ran down the events of the last few weeks. He was impressed. She had gotten close to the cult leader, Christopher Hewiston, but could not meet the missing girl.

"You made it inside quickly."

"Yes. They have this little church in town closed off to everyone except members and prospects. This group of four guys leave the church to go out to a diner every Friday night, it's the only place in town. So I was there the next week at the same time. Opposite booths. One guy tried to chat me up, and we talked about the church. I told them I was visiting relatives nearby and was interested in meeting people."

"How you holding up?"

"Fine. I know I should have called you last night after the car followed me. I wasn't sure. I didn't want to make it a big deal."

"No need to be a hero. Keep in mind that these people are not to be underestimated. You should have been checking in each night."

"I know, Ray. I wanted to handle it."

Ray felt his blood rise. "This isn't a movie, Tania. People have gone missing there." Tania fell quiet. Ray shook his head and exhaled loudly. "Well, it's over. You did well. Let's go through what you learned."

"I got inside the compound three times. First time was the new member orientation, just a fifteen-minute talk on a bench outside the place. The kid who invited me—Bronson—was there, with some other kids. I kept it brief. I didn't want to come off too interested in these wackos."

"What happened next?"

"That was a special service on Saturday. That was the first time inside the compound. I saw him, Hewiston. He was walking into some kind of chapel. They took us into a conference room where a minister—Brother Tim was his name—led the service and asked the newcomers about their experiences on the search. That's kind of how they rope you in—'We're all searchers; the question is what will you find? Or will something find you?'"

"And no sign of the girl?"

"None. Hewiston lives in this special section of the compound. They fenced the entire area off, 24/7 security. There are all these signs that you cannot go see him without permission. He's called Father Christopher, that's the terminology. They take it seriously. I called him Brother Christopher on impulse once and the guys flipped!"

They talked it over and agreed that she had done everything she could. She was burned now, though. He would have to think about who else could infiltrate the group.

"Ray, I have to talk to you about something. Got an unexpected call from Dominique."

"She called you?" It surprised him it had come to this. His first thought was he should get angry. But all he felt was sadness.

"She wanted to check in with me, see how I was doing." She frowned. "I feel funny telling you this."

Ray sighed. "It's no secret. She doesn't think you're ready. She thinks I'm putting you in a dangerous situation."

Tania began laughing softly. "How quaint. I worked as an escort for the largest criminal group on the west coast and now she's worried."

Ray nodded. "She means well. It's just—I don't know. She doesn't want to see you get too involved with these kinds of people again."

She got quiet. "I know, I appreciate it. But she sounded very down. I don't know." She trailed off.

"What?"

"She said she doesn't see any sense in coming here. To Boston."

Ray sat quietly. So she told Tania this before telling him. "It seems she made a decision. She's reading into what happened between us. Or what didn't happen. It's tough for us right now."

"I am sorry."

"Not your fault. You did nothing wrong. Neither one of us did."

"It was a strange call. Kind of final."

Ray didn't know what to make of that comment. He let the moment pass. Tania looked out over the garden. He sipped his wine. "Well, it's time to bring you into something here as well." He told her about Davin Price, and her eyes grew animated.

CHAPTER 25

AFTER TANIA LEFT, Ray looked over the trial transcript one more time. The identification of Langford bothered him. The witness, Augustina Calderon, made a solid identification on Sam. Maybe a little too good. According to the police reports and trial transcripts, Augustina was walking on Summer Street at midnight. She had come from the bar where she and her boyfriend had been drinking. No other witness remembered seeing them inside the bar, however.

The prosecutor made his case around her identification. Her boyfriend never testified; he died from a heroin overdose a few weeks later. Shooting the white powder—not typically a sign of reliable witness testimony.

He had done some background research on Augustina. She was a lifelong Boston girl with criminal charges involving drugs and prostitution when she was younger. She had several criminal cases dismissed around the time of Langford's trial. Interesting timing. At the time of trial, she worked as a stripper. He wondered if she had moved on. He recalled a comment from a girl who worked in the trade; she had answered questions about a co-worker, "You think old strippers ever retire?"

Then he looked again at the name of the police officer who interviewed Augustina. Detective Cahill. Identical name of the cop who pulled him over the other night. Could it be the same guy? Maybe the police were tipped off on his work. He would have to be careful.

With renewed interest, he read through the key passages of the trial:

"So you saw this man on Summer Street, is that what you are saying?"

"Yes."

"What time was this?"

"Late at night. Just after last call."

"Do you see that man here today?"

"Yes."

"Can you point him out?"

"Let the record reflect the witness pointed to the defendant, Mr. Langford."

"Did you engage in any discussions with him in the bar?"

"No."

"What about outside the bar?"

"A few words. He said hello. Introduced himself."

"What did he say?"

"Said his name was Sam Langford. I remember

it because there was a diner near my house called Langfords."

Ray stopped and considered the absurdity of the ID. She saw Langford at 2:00 a.m., then spoke to him—a complete stranger—on a deserted street, the same man who had not bothered her in the bar. Then she nailed the coffin shut by telling the jury she remembered his name because she used to walk by a greasy chicken shack by that same name many years ago. All this from a drug addict who had trouble remembering her own name on nights when she told men it was Maura, Bianca, or whatever alibi she was lost in at that moment.

Augustina was living in Dorchester on the corner of Columbia Road and Massachusetts Avenue. Whatever the truth of her new life, her trial testimony smelled rank to him. He wondered why the defense lawyer had not looked at her harder. Someone had gotten to her, he was sure of it. Time for a walk-up interview. Ray didn't want her to lawyer up, so it was best to go see her unannounced. Some witnesses almost seemed to wait for it, waiting for a time when the whole mess would explode into the open. Interview work retained a lost simplicity. You knock, they talk. Or they don't. Some witnesses had a sense of larger forces in motion—trials, guilt, and innocence. Some didn't care.

The next morning, he took his coffee out to the car and meandered his way through Roxbury. The day promised to be scorching, and he dressed casually in jeans, loafers, and a white silk shirt. He parked and walked over to a new apartment building on the corner of Everett Square. Someone buzzed him in sight unseen, unusual for this neighborhood. Inside, he banged up the stairs, listening to his steps echo from the clattering stairwell. As he walked to the apartment, a rear door opened. A woman looked outside, a Latina with blonde highlights on long, dark hair. She wore a pink sweatshirt and yoga pants that showed off a lithe physique. He had first placed her in her mid-thirties until his gaze rested on her eyes again. They didn't fit the bones of her face; they were older, wary. Not unfriendly, but joyless.

"Augustina?" She nodded. "I'm Ray Infantino. I'm working on an old criminal case over in Superior Court."

"What's this about?"

"Can we sit down for a minute? This is the Sam Langford case."

She hesitated but said nothing, just opened the door to let him inside. The house was messy, boxes piled high on tables and chairs, the fridge pulled out from the wall as if someone was working on the motor. A glass tower of dirty dishes tottered near the sink.

She caught his gaze. "Please excuse the mess. How did you find me? I just moved in here."

"Databases, nothing unusual."

"Okay." She shifted in her seat. "This is about the bar, right? The murder."

So she remembered. "Yes. Sam Langford's case."

"I've said everything I can say on it."

"Sure, I know." Ray looked at her again. A tough, defiant little thing, but something vulnerable hidden deep behind her eyes. She had a mild tremble in her leg, maybe nerves. Maybe something else. "You remember it?"

"Sure, yeah, I went to court on it. Why do I need to talk about it again?" She got up and started moving boxes off the table.

"Do you want to get a coffee down the street?"

"No, I was just making some." She reached into a box and emerged with a turquoise mug in her hand. "You want a cup?"

"That would be great, thank you."

She fixed them a pot of coffee and got out milk and a package of sugar. She moved briskly, but it didn't mask that tremor in the leg.

"Sam Langford is my client. He's been in prison since the trial."

"That's a long time ago."

"Yes. He's never changed his story. He says he's innocent. And I believe him."

He watched her absorb it. "Mmm hmm," she muttered.

"Tell me a little about the time the police interviewed you. How did they come to find out you had seen him at the bar?"

Augustina squinted at her cup of coffee as if trying to decipher tiny writing on the side. She was stalling. "I was at the bar. This was the night before I met the police. I had heard about the murder, guys were talking at the bar. So I called the station to tell them." She paused. "What I saw."

"So you called them first."

"Yes."

Ray nodded. "Interesting. What happened next?"

"I met with them. They came to my house."

"Where was this?"

"I... I don't remember where I was. I moved a lot in that period. Must have been my house, the place in Dorchester I was living at."

"So what did you tell them?"

"I was at the bar and I saw that man outside. He was inside earlier in the night and we talked for a minute. He was talking to the girl, walking to his car."

"What time was this?"

"Closing." She got up and tossed some newspapers into a pile on the floor.

"Who was the cop who interviewed you?"

"I don't remember."

"A Detective Cahill and his supervisor, Magnus, signed off on the report. Ring a bell?"

Her face was flat, expressionless. "I don't know those names. It's been so long."

"I'll read it to you. The report says, 'Officers after canvassing the bar took a statement from Augustina Calderon.' So it sounds like they interviewed you at the bar."

He paused, but she said nothing.

"Or took a statement. That's what cops like to call it."

She brushed her hair back with a fierce push. "I might be mistaken. Whatever the report says is probably right."

Ray ran through the report point by point, going over things in detail. She thought she talked to the man in the bar, but Ray showed her the trial transcript where she said she never met him. She squirmed around on certain points and deferred to the report. As they went on, Augustina looked agitated and sad at the same time. Still, she made no move to toss him.

"Look, I know it has been many years since this trial," said Ray. "All the little details, the when and where, they get fuzzy. But interesting that it was Magnus who interviewed you. How was he with his questioning?"

Augustina turned her shoulder toward him and pulled the boxes down absentmindedly. "He was a dick. But they all are."

"Magnus once worked with a cop named Gatling, who I investigated a few years back. Gatling's in prison now. Abusing witnesses. Female witnesses were his specialty."

At that, Augustina turned toward him slightly.

"He raped female informants. Then it all caught up with him."

Ray took a slow draught of coffee. He could feel her eyes blazing into him.

"What happened?" she said. "How did they get him?"

"A woman came forward in this case. She worked as an informant for many years. He raped her and threatened her if she told anyone. But she found her strength. Women always do, even if it takes a while."

She looked down to the floor and said nothing. Ray spoke to her a bit more about the report, but she wasn't able to recall any details—it seemed like a road to nowhere.

"This woman," Augustina blurted out, "who was she?"

"She was a working girl at the time. Now she's out of that life. She faced him down in court."

Augustina tossed a box on the floor and stood in the middle of the floor. A faraway look rose in her dark eyes. She wasn't even in the room anymore. Ray sat patiently. "Can you tell me? What did these two cops do?"

Her voice was firm. "I told them where I was that night. Told them the truth. Nowhere near that bar." Her mouth curled up. "But they didn't like it."

"What did they do then?"

"Do what they always do. Kept at me. Pressuring me to say certain things."

"Like what?"

"First the one in uniform pulled me out of the club one night. Drove around like a crazy man, saying that someone's looking for me and they were chasing us. It seems stupid now, but it was so real.

What kind of cop would do this to someone? I didn't doubt it was true. Plus, I had my own troubles."

"And how many times did he see you, the one named Magnus?"

She sighed. "I don't know who that is. But there were two of them, a cop in uniform and a plain-clothes guy."

"What did the plainclothes guy look like?"

"Sharp face, kinda narrow, ratty eyes. Just creepy feeling from the first time I met him." She paused. "I got arrested for shoplifting one night. The plain-clothes detective showed up then. They took me for a ride down to Roxbury."

Augustina's eyes faded out, and she went silent. She took a sip of coffee.

"And they wanted you to put Langford there at the bar?"

She sighed. "Yes. I was so drugged up then that I didn't really remember where I was. I mean I did, but…" She trailed off. She held her coffee and looked off into the distance. "It was easier to just go along with what they said. Look, I never saw your guy there, okay? That much I'm sure of. It was all bull-shit. I don't know where I was that night, but I can say this: I know I was never at that bar."

Ray sat for a minute and Augustina wiped her wet face with the back of her hand.

"I always knew someone would come around asking about this. Someone like you." She sighed.

"I'm sorry he's still in prison. I was afraid but I don't care anymore what they do to me."

"Nothing stays buried forever, Augustina. It all comes out eventually."

Augustina let out a deep breath. Something seemed to let go of her, and her face looked less fractured. "I'll tell you everything I know."

PART 4

AUGUSTINA'S TALE

1997

CHAPTER 26

AUGUSTINA CALDERON DROVE up Route 1 past the bottleneck near Malden where the roadway swerved and tossed drivers into a sharp turn. Never easy making a living. Even north of Boston, the rents were crazy high. Her two kids stayed with her baby-daddy on Friday nights so she could pull a full shift at the Golden Banana. Last week, the manager installed steel cages that rotated over the stage. Rumor was this was groundbreaking stuff in California strip clubs. The cages dropped from the ceiling and the strippers went inside and gyrated inside the cage. Nude women in cages that dropped from the ceiling had real earning power; she heard some of the other girls bragging about making triple the cash from a floor show.

Route 1 was Boston's version of the Las Vegas strip, a tacky 1950s-era highway lined with down-low motels, neon night clubs, and restaurants. It had a larger-than-life vibe—a replica Leaning Tower of

Pisa, a giant cactus at the old Hilltop Steakhouse complete with plastic cows grazing outside. But the highway's heyday was fading. Chain restaurants and furniture stores popped up along Route 1 as it lost its aura of glitzy fun and began to look like a thousand other lifeless shopping malls. Only a few strip clubs remained.

Augustina drove past the Nova Motel, where a white fence rotted next to a cockeyed vacancy sign. A man was touching up the paint on the shingles, makeup for a caved-in façade. A sign for the strip club, a cement building with a yellow awning and neon sign, loomed behind the motel: *Cage Dancing, World Famous Golden Banana.*

In the ladies dressing room, the mingled scents of dollar store perfume wafted throughout the air. Heavy metal pumped out like a sonic snake on the sound system. The girls chattered in loud voices about the two-legged ATMs out there. It was time to de-cash some dudes.

The afternoon dragged into night. After dancing a few songs, Augustina walked outside to smoke a cigarette. She wore thigh-high white boots with thick six-inch heels she had purchased from a transvestite shop owner in the South End. She set the boots off with a pink bikini. She felt good because she looked good. Ghettofab. And the Percs she got from one of her regulars was making the night slide by on a narcotic carpet ride. Maybe he would be in tonight. Even from here, she could smell the pent-up lust inside the club. Men, it was so easy to figure them out.

Augustina's dance shift came around and she strode out onto the stage. She saw one of her regulars, Mike, the fence installer down the road who liked to eat dinner with the strippers. She could see his head pumping slowly in sync with "You Got Another Thing Coming" by Judas Priest. Mike loved the hot ALL-YOU-CAN-EAT buffet, back lit in neon, especially the chicken wings. He usually made it a long night. She went over, danced, and collected some tips.

As she came off stage, Cristal strode over. "There's that cop waiting for you again. He's in the lobby. Sorry, baby." She walked out to the stage. Augustina sighed and left the dressing room.

There he was again. He was a big guy, this cop, standing by the door. Seemed agitated. Customers gave him a wide berth. She moved toward him. "You need to talk to me again?"

"Yes, Augustina. I'm Officer Cahill."

She nodded. "Boston PD, right?"

He leaned a mottled cheek down toward her. "Yes. You now have a Boston problem."

"I got a shift coming up, I can't talk now."

"Probably best to cancel." He leaned toward her and said in a low voice, "Someone's looking for you."

"What?"

"You don't want to get found by these guys."

"Who are you talking about?" He motioned

toward the door for her to follow. She trotted after him. "You're freaking me out here," she said.

"No joke, we gotta get you out of here."

"Why? Who—"

"Get in." He held open the door of his cruiser. The backseat was empty.

"I need to know what this is about," Augustina yelled. She stepped into the backseat. The car lurched forward, and she shot back into the hard backseat. "Christ, take it easy will ya—"

"I think under the circumstances, my driving is the least of your concerns." She saw his eyes loom in the rearview. "We got word that some people are looking for you. You're in danger. This is all for you," he said, gesturing to the dashboard.

"Who? What are you talking about?"

The cop said nothing. He drove on Route 1 south and turned off near a giant orange dinosaur at a mini-golf place in Malden. He pulled into the parking lot of a nightclub lit in neon green. Across the street was an industrial lot bursting with trailers.

Cahill turned to look at her. "The girl who was murdered at the bar. Word is that you saw something. Now certain people are trying to get—"

A car pulled up close behind the cruiser. The rear window exploded with white light.

The cruiser leapt to life as Cahill pushed the accelerator to the floor. Augustina cried out in surprise as the car bottomed out in a rut, her head caroming off the headrest.

"This is who I'm talking about," said Cahill, turning hard to the left and sending her careening along the back bench until she braced her leg on the front seat.

"Why are we running?"

The cruiser bombed down route 99 toward the city, slamming off the rutted pavement. They went past a Brazilian store painted in green and yellow. Cahill drove in silence.

She looked back and saw a car following them. Cahill rattled across the Malden Bridge over the Mystic River. She got tossed again and nearly knocked her head into the right window. No one drove like this. Who were these people?

There was a car, maybe more than one, right behind them, beeping wildly, flashing high beams at the cruiser. The cop kept the gas pedal pinned.

"Keep your head down until I tell you we're clear." Cahill's face furrowed in concentration. A horn ripped, and a siren blared. The cruiser surged forward. Augustina felt lightheaded. If someone came out of a side street, they'd be dead.

The cruiser turned hard into a parking lot and she felt it lurch up on the edge of its tires. She screamed. The cruiser slid sideways in a cloud of gravel and accelerated back onto the roadway.

"You're a cop, can't you do something!"

Cahill spoke calmly. "We will not let these guys get to you, Augustina." The cop hit a turn hard and barreled through a pot hole. "The people who you talked with that night—"

"My God, I told you, I don't even know what you're talking about!"

"We're not going there, Augustina!" The cop shouted, still driving fast. "We know you were at the bar."

She opened her mouth to say something, but stopped when the cop raised a hand as if he would backhand her across the mouth. Wouldn't be the first time.

"Stay low." The high beams still played across the cruiser. She heard the hum of rubber tires on a steel bridge. She did as she was told, kept her head down and crouched down on the seat.

Eventually, the cruiser slowed and drove at a normal speed. Cahill got off and headed toward South Boston. She peered out the window and watched the tops of the skyscrapers slide by.

When she felt the car slowing, she looked around. They were near the waterfront. The cop pulled into a dim parking lot behind a squat office building. A granite block quay sagged into the water, the gravel base breaking down year after year under the crushing weight of the stone. There was nothing safe about this place, and she felt a wave of fear course throughout her body. She knew that bar the cops had been asking about was just down the corner. Were they going to take her in there? It was a rough place. A few blocks away, the power station loomed, a squat shadow above the gas-streaked harbor. There was no one nearby, the only sound the steady hum of the electric lines running through the blackness.

She felt a bruise on her shoulder where she had slid hard into the door. "What is this about?" The pills had worn off, and she needed something to calm her head.

"They are looking for you. These people, they've taken shots before at witnesses. They're willing."

"Jesus, who are these people?"

"Gang members, D Street projects. Lot of talk at the bars about this thing. You need to lie low. It's gonna be a long summer."

"I have a job."

"You should quit."

"How can I quit? I have children to support."

Cahill snorted. She sighed and sat back in the gloom. She could barely see his face, just criss-cross corners when the streetlights hit a bony cleft on his forehead, a piece of his mouth.

"I don't even know who you are—"

"I'm here for you, Augustina."

"Well, I don't really want to get involved in this. I hate court."

The half-lit face turned around, his voice low and tense. She could smell food on his breath, some kind of spicy meat. "We know you were there. You're not gonna back off that now. Don't lapse into your little drug world here. I mean, if you're thinking of ignoring everything we said and talked about, then I can tell you there are going to be some unhappy customers out there. You and your family need protection. You gotta come clean with us on what you saw. Let's start here: When did you first see this guy?"

He handed her a picture and turned on the overhead lights. She was looking at a face she had never seen in her life.

"I don't know him. Who is he?"

"Bad dude. With those people tonight..." Cahill's voice faded out and his hand waved at the darkness, dismissing the threat. "Those are his people."

"I don't think I ever saw this man."

"Take a better look at the guy. Explore the face a bit." Cahill waited and turned around again. "We have witnesses who say you had words with this guy that night."

"I wasn't there that night, I told you—"

Cahill whipped around, grabbed her wrist, and pulled her face close. She dropped the photograph to the floor. "Listen, cunty. You sell that pussy to anyone, and he was buying that night. That's the story. You're so slopped up most of the time, how the fuck would you remember?"

"I'm telling you—"

"Shut up a minute there, Augustina. Just answer my questions truthfully. A girl is dead. You owe us that much. When did you first get there—"

"I told you."

He raised his hand near her face. "No, you lied to me."

She slumped back in the seat, her heart thudding.

"Was this your idea or Anthony's? We know how he operates. Offer a ride to a drunk, you show some tits and ass, then you jack the guy up. His idea, wasn't it? He operates out of the place on weekends."

Augustina began screaming at him. Cahill shook his head in disgust. He started the car and drove back through Chelsea to the strip club.

Cahill leaned over the front seat and stared at her. "You got your kids to think about here. DSS will take a hard look at someone like you. Stripper, drug addict. Court cases up the ass. 'How does Augustina provide for these kids? How does she do it?' That's the question. Maybe a little something extra for her customers?"

Augustina felt sick to her stomach thinking of the cops coming into her home. She jumped out the backseat and raced back into the club.

CHAPTER 27

TWO DAYS AFTER Cahill's unpleasant visit, Augustina stepped inside the grocery store near Beacon Hill on the last billows of a methedrine haze. The store was one of the new places where they piled the fruits high, oranges and apples and peaches in little colorful hills, so lush she thought they could have a cover charge just to enter the joint. Not her usual place to shop, but a girl could look. She looked on in amazement. Good Lord, they even lined the fruit pile with real straw! She felt like a kid in a farmhouse. It was an illusion of plenty, a back-to-basics health that made her feel envious and joyful at the same time. She watched rich ladies in coordinated pastel outfits as they peeked at each apple or kiwi, testing for punctures or bruises, minor imperfections that meant a reject. Life was full of rejects. But there were no bruises on theses ladies, she could see that. Their lives were luscious cakes that she knew she would never taste.

Augustina walked to the meat aisle but, whoops—
she realized she forgot a shopping cart. She laughed a
bit to herself. She walked back, grabbed a cart, and
started shopping, tossing a few items into the basket
without looking at what she was picking up. Frosted
Flakes, crackers with built-in cheddar cheese, choc-
olate bars, blue-colored drinks, the staple crap of
an American diet. She walked back to the chests of
refrigerated meats.

She had smoked meth that morning with her boyfriend Anthony and now her head was coming down
hard and fast. Their dad would drop the kids off at
6 p.m. and she needed some food. Ice cream—it was
a rarity in her house. A treat for tonight. She reached
inside and grabbed something flavorful-looking,
something packed with candy and swirls of caramel.
She looked around the store at the checkout lanes.
Quite busy. Good.

She noticed some thick-cut steaks that would
fit right in her jeans. She tossed the steaks into the
cart. Then she took a T-bone, too; she always liked
to cook with the bone in because her mother told
her that's where the marrow was. And good people
should live close to the bone.

Augustina ran her hands through her scraggly
hair. She felt like hell. She needed a shower. Two ladies
cruised by and she smiled at them. They ignored her.
Screw them, nose-in-the-air bitches. She wheeled the
carriage to the dog food aisle where it was quieter.
Looking around, she lifted up her white blouse and

crammed the package of steaks down her pants. So far so good. The T-bone went in next—whoa, it was cold! She pulled the blouse back over her pants. God, she should've put the steaks in a plastic bag so the juice wouldn't run down her leg. Christ, it would be embarrassing if red streaks ran down on her pant leg at the cashier. She could tell them she was having her period. She laughed again to herself.

"Mr. Jenkins, please report to the front desk," came over the intercom. Who the hell was Mr. Jenkins? As Augustina walked by the frozen waffle freezer, she looked at herself—her jeans were so tight the meat tray was bulging out and ruining her figure. She was proud of her slim figure. Her mother told her she should be. She should use her figure while she had one because men did things for skinny girls with big tits. But a good figure did not last forever. Neither did the men.

A little girl sidled by and stared at her. Was she looking at the steaks in her underpants? Augustina was not sure. The coolness of the meat felt good against her skin.

It was time to blow this clambake. She left the cart in the aisle and headed for the exit. She had nearly made it through the door when a man stepped in front of her, not big, but businesslike, a serious set to his face, rippling muscles in his forearms.

"I'm David Jenkins from the security department. Would you just step aside here? We have you on video placing some items on your person and leaving the store without paying."

She moved toward the wall and thought she might faint. She thought about making a run for the doors, but she knew she wouldn't get too far with a steak down her leg. She walked with the man to a back office.

An hour later, Augustina was scratching at her face, agitated and scared. Her head was drifting around a windowless office and she needed to jolt her nervous system to a better place. Needed to ratchet her head back on. Anything would work: a nicotine hit, a caffeine jolt, a meth binge, a little weed—just get her the hell out of this office.

They stuck some papers in front of her to read and she signed, admitting to the theft. Augustina gave fingerprints to a guy who came in, a young kid who was staring at her tits and gulping nervously. She stood for a photo. She didn't smile. All that court stuff made her crazy. She told the security guy, "I'm not ready for court."

After she had signed the papers, they even made her give back the steaks.

Another hour of this crap dragged by. Her head pulsed with a dull ache. Then a cop walked in the room. It was Cahill, the cop who had come to the club two days ago. She froze. He was talking to the head security guy. He looked over at her once too often with a wolfen gaze that unsettled her. Tiny hairs on her neck bristled when she heard him finish.

"I'll take her down and book her." Cahill smiled as he walked toward her. She stood wordlessly. Then he walked her to the cruiser, holding her arm with a firm grip. He shoved her head down as she got into the backseat.

In the backseat, she looked over with surprise at a man sitting next to her. He was dressed in a blazer, black dress pants, and thick-soled shoes. But what caught her attention was his flat, reptilian face, with tiny, intense eyes above a tight mouth that looked like it cracked open only partway. Not given to friendly smiles. She took an instant dislike to him. The store security guys were one thing, serious but harmless. This guy looked like something else entirely. He said nothing, just looked her over like she was a slab of meat ready for the fire.

Cahill got in and the cruiser took off. "Boosting steaks, Augustina? You are beautiful, honey."

"Fuck you."

"Oh, that filthy mouth," Cahill mocked her. "You suck your daddy off with that thing too?"

She sat back, no point in arguing. The man next to her sat without saying a word. He didn't even seem to hear the conversation. Finally, she could not take it any longer and she turned to face him.

"So, you're a cop too, right?" No answer. She tried to draw him out. "Why are you just sitting here?"

The guy just stared out the window. Cold, cold eyes. Then Cahill interrupted from the front seat. "You're dumb, that's why. It's your destiny."

"Geez, that's classy," she hissed at Cahill. "Fuck off."

Cahill laughed, and she turned away to look out the window. Her headache was getting worse. They drove out of downtown and took the exit for Massachusetts Avenue. She saw a metal sign for Victoria's Diner and then they turned onto a deserted industrial road into Roxbury. A chain-link fence ran along a junkyard up ahead. She didn't know this area, an isolated section of Boston filled with empty lots, squat warehouses, and rutted asphalt. The cruiser pulled off the road into the yard of a brick warehouse with faded white letters running across one side.

"Augustina, where were you last Saturday night?" The plainclothes cop—Steelface, that was who she decided he was. He was talking, finally. He stared at her.

"Saturday. I'm not sure—"

"Think, please. Take a minute."

"Wait. I dunno. I was with Anthony last weekend. Because I know my kids were with their dad."

"Your kids? The loads you should have eaten, Augustina," he said. Cahill laughed.

Augustina stared at him, unsure where this guy was going. He was a creep. She needed to keep the world at bay. She rubbed her eyes, tried to focus. She looked outside and saw a few cars bounce down Southampton. It was dead quiet in the warehouse lot.

"Let me check your phone."

She paused. Maybe this would speed it up. She handed over her phone.

The cop took her phone, a basic flip phone. He looked at it, dialed someone, and let it ring. Then he covered the mouthpiece after listening to whoever picked up. Augustina looked around. Then he handed it back.

"It is your phone, right?"

"Yes."

"Were you in South Boston last week?"

"No. I stayed down here with Anthony."

"We found your number calling into a phone linked to the murder."

"Oh my God!"

"A witness came in and rolled on you. She saw you and a guy at the bar in Southie, the Electric House."

"Oh my God, come on!"

"Look at me."

"You gotta believe me, I wasn't near that place—" She shook her head. God, she felt like crap. She needed a cigarette, something to calm her nerves.

"It was a setup. Anthony and his friend, robbing drunks. The only question is, how did you help plan it, Augustina? What was your cut?"

The plainclothes cop went at her for over an hour, lancing her story over and over until she was not sure what she was agreeing or disagreeing with. His voice had a low, cutting sound that unnerved her. He slashed at her confidence, fragile as it always was, and she felt like she was tumbling down an open sewer. She wasn't certain, if she was to be honest, where she was that night. Drinking and drugging were burning her memory out. Like acid on metal, everything became a foamy mess.

"I don't think we were anywhere near that place, sir. You gotta believe me." Then again, maybe she was. A long, blurry train of lost Saturday nights. The cop said they just wanted to put away a murderer. Was that so bad? "Can I go? I'd like to get out here."

"You sure? We'll let you off somewhere safe."

She looked at the cop next to her with a question in her eyes.

The cop said nothing, just reached across and opened the rear door on his side. He didn't move, though. Augustina had to step over his leg. As she did so, she felt his hand invade her, sliding up inside the crease of her legs. So it was gonna be that way. Then he reached over to pull her back and slammed the door shut.

Cahill turned around from the driver's seat and handed her a bottle of wine. "No cups, honey," he said, smirking. "Right from the bottle. Didn't think you'd mind. Just a few more questions."

Augustina ignored the jibe and took the bottle. A California wine, a pinot noir. Shit, this was excellent shit, better than the bottom-shelf grape juice she usually drank. And she needed a drink right now.

"Have a sip. It'll calm you down."

Augustina looked at the bottle, shook it a little, listened to the sloshing of the seductive red. She felt a little piece of her head drift on a longing tide. She was planning to get into a rehab program. She shouldn't have any liquor here. She knew better, especially with these animals next to her. But the day was lost. She had smoked earlier that day, so what was one more? They could violate her probation. Her throat felt dry as desert sand. She reached out.

"Well, just one drink."

Her trembling fingers wrapped tighter around the swamp-green bottle. She sipped. Sipped again. Drew the sweet poison deep into her throat. This was what she needed. Just take off the edge. She could hear Cahill breathing deeply; he was one of those noisy-lung dudes. The plainclothes cop sat next to her, staring out the window at nothing in particular. The bottle hit her lips again. She needed the wine right now, she had to out-think these cops. The alcohol coursed through her body.

"So, Augustina, that Saturday when you were at the bar. Where did you see him standing?"

"Near the bar?"

"Listen to my question. Yeah, the bar. The bar where you drank that night. This is the bar, the Electric House." He held a photo toward her and she saw a dive bar with small smoked-glass windows.

Sure that was the place, what difference did it make anyway? The goddamn guy killed a girl.

The plainclothes cop snakelicked her with his soft voice. He asked so many questions, and some of them were good. She sipped and sipped from the bottle. Maybe it was a new bottle. The label looked different even if the wine tasted the same.

The cop got close to her face and his rancid breath made her want to vomit. He stared at her.

"A word from us, your kids are gone. Probably better for them. Some people would say, 'What kind of upbringing can a whore give to her kids?' I'm not that guy, Augustina. I don't sit in judgment. I just investigate homicides."

She felt sick as an old memory rose in her mind. They could take her son and daughter over this. They had done it once before. Her weakness, the dance she did each day with the pills or weed or whatever else was around. Her little babies, the only reason she laid on her back and let strange men grind out their lust on her body. God, if they took her kids, the last five years would be meaningless. And that was too much.

The detective was staring at her with ice-blue eyes. "Time to get on the right side of things, Augustina. For once in your life. It could be a new beginning for you. Make some friends in the right places." He took out a photo from his jacket pocket. "I want you to look at this picture. This is Sam Langford. He killed the girl. How certain are you this is the guy at the bar? Now that you've had a chance to reflect."

Augustina felt a tide of revulsion roll inside her. For them, for all of it. She took the photograph in her hands and looked at the face for a long, long time. It was dark and quiet on the edge of town.

"This is him," she said finally. "I'm sure of it." The detective spoke more words, but she didn't understand.

Her head felt better now, and the wine lit up a warm feeling behind her face. She maybe had one drink too many. She felt it was time to leave.

Then the detective leaned over, reached for her arm, and pulled her toward him. He moved his mouth to her neck and put his hand between her legs. She shook her head. "Come on, guys—"

The detective held her arm as Cahill shoved the bottle at her again. She felt the wine bottle pressed against her mouth and a small stream of wine ran down her neck. Jesus, they were all the same. They wanted her to go along. And she felt she should. The guy was pressing her so hard the bottle smashed off her tooth.

The big man, Cahill, shifted in the front seat, laughing. There was a hand on her breast, squeezing so hard she felt like crying. Some men were like this; they wanted forceful, dirty ceremonies. The sex had to be brutish because this was what they were, the essence of them.

"Okay, guys, just take it easy—"

Augustina was doing so good now. Her kids were almost out of school and not getting in trouble. She and Anthony were not fighting anymore. She would not wreck this over a romp in the backseat. Augustina slipped her hands down to the cop's pants and undid the buckle. She could play the game. The detective held her by the neck and mounted her. The car bounced and shimmied. She floated away again on a chemical carpet ride. It was over quickly. After a few minutes, the detective sighed and finished. He let go of her neck. She sat up. Cahill was up next, saying it was his turn. And then it was over.

The detectives told her they would be in touch. They needed her for the trial. Then the rear door of the cruiser opened up and Augustina stumbled out. The cruiser slid out to Massachusetts Avenue and headed back downtown. Augustina walked down the dark sidewalk.

An hour later, the red mist was dissipating. Since the two pigs did their thing. Augustina thought of that word: pigs, pigshit, pigmen raping her in a police cruiser.

Augustina stumbled up past the meatpacking warehouses, just a shadow while the stars wheeled overhead and starlight oozed like pus from holes in the firmament. She wanted a white rose and got a nasty surprise, as her momma used to say. She looked out toward the lights of the downtown towers, a thousand yellow cat-eyes staring at her from a distance. She had no idea how far she had to walk to reach those lights. They looked close, but she knew better. Tonight, the city existed for everybody but her.

PART 5

PAST IS PRESENT

CHAPTER 28

MAGNUS WALKED INTO police headquarters on Tremont Street with his usual morning coffee. June had been a hot month and bodies were piling up around the city: petty gang disputes, retaliatory hits, the occasional domestic stabbing. It never changed.

He would head down to the Cape for the weekend. He had bought a house in Yarmouth two decades ago and taken out a mortgage. But the mortgage was just for show. Fact was, he could have paid cash. He had two safes in the basement bursting with cash. Sometimes he went down there late at night just to feel the money, run it through his hands. There was cash from the whores. Cash from dealers his men had smashed. Cash from fake search warrants, where they busted down some suburban drug dealer, took his cash, and warned him to piss off and shut his trap. And there were the proceeds from his clients in Southie, close to a decade of payments for the tips that led to the demise of the Mafia.

Law enforcement paid well in the Commonwealth.

Cahill had texted him earlier: The chief wanted to see them. He met Cahill in the cafeteria.

"What's the old prick want now?"

"No idea."

Magnus shook his head, and they headed up to see the Chief of the Boston Police Department, Robert F. Quinn. He was always called Chief Quinn, or Robert to his friends—never Bob or, Lord forbid, Bobby. He had been in command since Magnus and Cahill came on the force. A West Roxbury townie, Quinn began his police career working summers as a special, as they called it way back when the chief could hand out a badge and deputize any bumpkin with half a brain and a ton of blind loyalty. Quinn had come up through that system and saw that the tree continued to grow. He was all about placing his boys in spots where they could pull the levers of power for him. And he had his boys everywhere.

Quinn had seen it all, preserving something of the old ways even in this late century. He was there for the barren years of the 1980s, before the city's revival, when crack poisoned the neighborhoods like a needle to the heart and channeled profits to Intervale Posse and the gangs off of lower Blue Hill Avenue. The gangs grew so bold that one gangster assassinated a district attorney at a train station. Politicians looked hard at the once-great city sprawled like a junkie in an alley, fallen into an urban nadir. Then the city began a slow, uneven revival.

Quinn had been one chief in the right place at the right time. Federal money flooded in to fight the gangs. Soon, the expanding gentrification of the South End and Fenway led to rising property taxes—and rising numbers of police to patrol it. Quinn had run the department for close to thirty years and was proud of maintaining an excellent relationship with the Irish mob that ran the DA's office.

Magnus and Cahill walked into the office. Cahill looked apprehensive. Magnus kept his back rigid as a ramrod. He just ignored Quinn's meddling.

Quinn gestured to some chairs by his desk and got right to the point. "An assistant DA from the Conviction Integrity unit called me today. Defense lawyer is asking questions about the Katie Donnegan murder case. Key witness was a woman, a stripper named Augustina Calderon. Supposedly, a PI interviewed her. Ray Infantino. He got Ms. Calderon to recant her testimony." He looked at Magnus. "She is raising some serious allegations. You closed this case. What do you remember about her?"

"Not much. That's an old case. I'd have to look at the case file."

"Do you recall talking to a female witness by that name?"

Magnus shook his head.

"Well, the point is, she claims the arresting officers abused her—you two."

"Chief, she's a stripper, they always go south,"

said Magnus. "Witnesses like her always do. These PIs get them to say anything."

"She is pretty specific in her allegations. Says a uniformed officer drove her from a strip joint on Route 1. And that you raced all over the place with her claiming you were being chased by someone." He glanced at Cahill.

"This is ridiculous. How many years ago was this?" Cahill asked.

"Fifteen." Quinn continued. "She says that summer, she got taken downtown after a shoplifting incident. Uniformed officer and a detective. Then she was raped somewhere near the South End."

Magnus said nothing, but Cahill's red face was telling. He looked fit to burst. "This is bullshit, Chief."

The chief sat back. "I will need your files on this case. Everything. Not just the reports you submitted to the CO. Do a desk search. I don't want this thing blowing up because you left a report in your drawer."

The men got up to leave. Magnus looked at Quinn. "We're fine on this, Chief. She's lying. These types. No one takes the word of a girl like this seriously."

Quinn frowned and walked close to Magnus. Even though he was three inches taller, Magnus knew there was trouble brewing as he looked down into the chief's dark eyes.

"Did you ever see her outside of an official investigation?"

Magnus shook his head no.

"Ever see her outside the station?"

"No, I don't think so."

"We will not have any further surprises here, gentlemen," said Quinn, turning back to his desk. "This department got smeared with Gatling's federal conviction. Enough! I don't want to handle any more shitstorms. Let me know when something's coming."

CHAPTER 29

McBain took the call at the bar. Magnus' voice on the line sounded angry. He insisted they meet right away—no phones. McBain knew what the deal was. No cells, no surveillance, no wiretap. Magnus told him to meet at Castle Island out by the bridge.

The urgency surprised McBain. He went home and changed into jogging shorts and a Bruins t-shirt. His leg still showed the scars from an old injury, but what the hell did he care if people stared at it? He walked outside and headed toward Castle Island. Underneath the roar of the jets over Boston Harbor, they could talk with the privacy they needed. Jet engines were great for screwing up a wiretap.

He began walking around Pleasure Bay. A gorgeous sunny day, a slight breeze in from the Atlantic. Why would anyone want to leave this place? He slowed at the agreed-upon spot, the outermost point of the crescent where the sea slid under the bridge and sucked at the rocks as it ran out into the open ocean. The afternoon crowd walked and talked in small groups under the roar of the jets.

McBain watched a figure walking toward him. He barely recognized Magnus' face. He had not seen the man in a few years, and time had been no friend to him. He appeared much older than his years, hollowed out. But McBain saw that Magnus' eyes still held that look, predatory and pitiless. McBain turned back the way he had come and fell into step with Magnus.

Magnus, as usual, was blunt. "A ghost came back."

"Which one?"

"That guy at the pub. Killed the blonde about fifteen years ago."

This caught McBain off guard. He didn't like being reminded of his moment of bad temper. He had buried that night deep down inside a long time ago. He had arranged everything. For the fall guy, Sam Langford, they had developed two witnesses who put him right at the scene. He couldn't believe there was anything to worry about. Business was steady, and old bones stayed buried.

"Why now?" McBain asked.

"Witness is getting a better memory. You remember the stripper?"

McBain snorted, "For Christ's sake!"

A group of old ladies strolled by, hands pumping, one with small weights in her hands. Magnus waited a beat until they were past. "She went to the DA, so the Conviction Integrity unit will raise hell. It's going to be fuck city over here. IA will be hard up my ass."

They fell silent as an obese woman in pink shorts slogged by. Her shorts had the word "bootylicious" emblazoned across the back.

"Shit, can't tell her ankles from her feet," muttered Magnus. The woman moved on down the path toward the star-shaped granite walls of Fort Independence. "There is a private investigator working on Langford's case. Check him out. Anyone we know can deliver a message to him, do it. But more important, and probably easier—get her to back off. Have a heart to heart with this girl."

"Consider it done."

"She was a whore and a drug addict. Worked one of the jack shacks on Route 1. No one believed her then, anyway. I'm not sure what she thinks she's doing by coming out now. We need to contain this. They might have her under protection, so just check out her situation for now."

They talked for a few minutes before another large group of walkers approached.

"Get it done," said Magnus.

"What about the other choice witness they called? Butters?"

"I expect he'll get a visit from this PI. See him yesterday. Make sure he knows what's happening. He needs to be on top of his story."

The sun blazed above the harbor. Families

picnicked on the grass and the line at Sullivan's was already a dozen deep. They stopped to look at the sea.

"Sox shit the bed last night," said McBain.

"Yeah."

"The bullpen sucks."

"We need a flamethrower. These guys we have now, they're all junk." Magnus gave him a tight smile. "Where's the appreciation for the classic verities?"

"That's right." McBain knew Magnus was driving home a point: There was no turning back now. Butters was the weak link. McBain needed to step on his neck.

Magnus turned and walked back the way he had come.

McBain felt like he had been dismissed. With some irritation, he considered how things had changed. Fifteen years ago, his crew had owned the young Magnus. He covered their ass when they told him so. But Magnus had risen through the ranks and now it was tough to tell who was bossing things. When the call came in earlier, Magnus had spoken to him like he was a rookie cop, a flunky.

McBain shook his head, turned the other direction, and sauntered back toward the fort.

CHAPTER 30

BUTTERS GOT DRESSED for a 10 a.m. check-in with his probation officer. Good guy, Tim Carter, a Mick from West Roxbury, who got the job a few years after he crashed his car into a guardrail at midnight under murky circumstances. Lucky for him, his uncle was a state representative. The police reports were filled out incorrectly. Then they never existed. While they filed no charges, the press got hold of the story and Carter ended up losing his court officer gig. He got shuffled over to probation, a friendly gesture from a friend on Beacon Hill. Butters saw sad days ahead. Boston was changing and the Gaelic sun was setting. The end of an era was on the horizon, and there were rumors they were going to make sure candidates were actually qualified to land a probation gig. Blood loyalty was the first casualty of modernism.

The sun was shining and Butters figured he'd stretch his legs. He took the long way to the probation office, walking by Boston Garden past the sports bars on Canal Street before heading to the courthouse for the sitdown with Carter.

Inside the probation office, his story matched the décor—beige and banal. He told Carter all the right things. Prospects looking up, applications submitted (all online, he was internet savvy). He was doing great and staying off the pills. It was a double-condom life for him now. Carter bought the story wholesale. Butters appreciated how Carter never busted his ass, seeming to sense in him the crust of a life he was chewing himself.

Butters finished the meeting in twenty minutes, no problems. He stopped for a cup of coffee and headed over to the North End. He sat down on a brass bench in the Greenway to watch the day pass. A blonde girl walked by. For a second, his heart iced over—her face looked like Susan O'Neil's.

He still thought of her. They had come up together in Dorchester, went to school during the lost years. He walked her into the school each day like a playground knight. He had a crush on her when they were little kids.

Butters used to stare at Susan's hair when he sat behind her in class. Her hair flowed down in a dusky blonde waterfall, so pure he could still visualize her face like she was right in front of him. She had once told him she liked a certain brand of shampoo, an aquamarine color. He could never forget the scent of her hair, the cleanest, freshest thing ever. He had heard that true love comes early in life when you're not ready; you're convinced that someone better is out there. Then life does its dirty work on you, and the old dreams burn to ashes.

Years later, he ran into her unexpectedly at a party in the Fenway. They were excited to see each other. She was the same sweet girl, while he was taking the path to nowhere, a street-level dealer with a high-end addiction. He felt so happy when he introduced her to it for the first time, some of the best meth he had gotten. Two hours later, her face swelled, her heart stopped, and she never regained consciousness. Everyone kept their mouth shut about the source, so there was never a problem with police. But something withered inside him, as sure as dark comes after sunset. And darkness became a longtime friend who never went away.

How long ago was it now? Over a dozen years since she passed.

Butters looked over at two women as they lathered on suntan lotion and laid towels out on the grass of the Greenway, a serpentine oasis amid the glass towers. This was when Boston was best, mid-summer: the heat almost southern, a tropical wetness on most days, girls out everywhere, tan python legs stretching on the pathways. The scent of fresh bread rose up from behind him—a guy hauling bags bursting with loaves from a North End bakery.

A shadow to his left interrupted his reveries. He glanced up. Tommy McBain was standing there, an unlit cigarette in his hand. The image startled Butters.

McBain was a demon, a whiff of sulphur, always there when least expected. He wore a faded black concert t-shirt with jeans and dark sunglasses. McBain kept a chiseled, muscular look every bit as hard as Butters remembered, like fire had run its course, burned off the excess, and left just sinew and bone.

"So, look what the wind brings. How you been, Joey?"

"I'm doing good, Tommy, good. How 'bout you?" He felt uneasy around McBain; he was always unpredictable. He reached out to shake McBain's hand.

"What brings you downtown, Joey?"

"Just out walking," said Butters.

"Still checking in with the man?"

Butters wondered if McBain had followed him from the courthouse. "Yeah, still on probation, you know."

"Sure." McBain sat down and looked around the park. "Haven't seen you around much, Joey. Where you been?"

"Just keeping my nose clean."

"This is good to hear." The men sat and talked and watched some tourists cross over to the stalls in Faneuil Hall. The younger one had a paper hat on his head, some goofball prank at one of the tourist restaurants.

Butters felt McBain looking over at him behind his shades. "Sox were not so good last night. But

Ortiz has got a few more seasons in him. Dude is jacked."

"Yeah, I hear ya. And they look primed in the pen this year."

Tommy puffed away on his cigarette and tossed the butt. "Listen, a guy come out to see you recently? A PI?"

Butters froze. So this was what the talk was all about. He wasn't sure how to answer. "No," he lied. "Why would he?"

"We're having a problem with him down at the bar."

"I didn't know."

"We're hearing some things about an old case involving the pub. Old murder case."

Butters said not a word.

"You remember the girl. There might be some appeal coming up."

"I didn't hear that."

"Yeah. Keep an eye out for this guy. Infantino is his name."

Butters stared straight ahead. "Sure."

McBain smoked a little and said nothing. "We need to be careful about this thing. We're keeping an eye out. How you remember this thing, what happened, all that has to check out."

"Yeah, sure. You got no problems with me."

"I know that, Joey. Because we do your remembering for you."

"You know I'm good, Tommy." He thought back

to how McBain had told him this years ago. They owned his memories.

McBain's face grew tight, and Butters wasn't sure if he had said something wrong. He could feel tension in McBain. It made him nervous.

Then McBain stood up, his right hand clenched in a fist. He opened it up. To Butters' relief, he saw it held a slip of paper. "You working these days, Joey?"

"Nah, not for a while."

"Call that number there." He shoved the paper at him. "A guy will connect you with some work. Deliveries around town, that kind of thing."

"Hey thanks, man, I appreciate. Been tough, you know. I apply somewhere..." he shrugged. "Never gets past the background check."

"Red flags, Joey! You got too many red flags!" McBain was laughing silently, his body shaking. "This guy, no background check needed. He's a friend from Dot Ave. He needs help with things from time to time."

Butters nodded. "Okay, Tommy, I'll call him."

He knew what that meant. A friend from Dot Ave worked the shady side of the street, and whatever job he had, it would not be just an office delivery. Butters pictured Susan's face again. What would she think of him now, mixing with a pure killer? But that was a long time ago, when a more innocent fire burned behind his eyes.

"I'm gonna head back, Tommy."

McBain nodded. "Take care of yourself, Joey. And call me if you hear anything."

Butters got up, and they shook hands. Butters walked toward the North End. He stopped at a crosswalk and casually looked back. McBain still sat there, a sinister, sculpted presence on the bench, eyeballing the world from behind sunglasses.

CHAPTER 31

ON A GRAY afternoon, Augustina watched the car drive back down the street. A Mercedes, white paint, tinted windows, something you see and admire and then forget on most days. But there it was again. Five times in one day. The car moved deliberately, a low-riding, cream-colored panther that looked almost sensuous in the way it moved down the street. Augustina's nerves were fraying. She needed an answer. Ever since she talked to Ray Infantino, the old problems were returning. She was sure something connected these cars to the police.

Years ago, during the investigation into the murder of the girl, she got used and discarded by those cops. Yesterday's trash blowing down the street. Cops who raped witnesses while hiding behind a badge. They made her sick. She later came to realize that these were men who didn't deserve the title of police officer; men who lacked the courage of even a simple thief, courage to admit what they were—outright criminals. They tore her down when she was already at the lowest place, using drugs, hooking at the club.

She had come so far. So why get involved with this mess again? But Infantino made a convincing case. An innocent man. She played the words over and over. Wasn't that the essence of living in this country? Freedom and an innocence that you did not have to prove? She couldn't let it go. Her lies were being used to keep a man in chains. She had buried that memory for years. Now that knowledge was leaching her guts out.

Mid-afternoon, she watched a man pass by, strolling up the street. She never saw him before on this street. Baseball cap with sunglasses on an overcast day. She had seen him somewhere before. Was he from the club? He seemed to slow down near the apartment lot and peered down the driveway.

The old waves of fear came rushing in again. She drew the shades. She put on some Outkast and smoked a little weed to kill off the nerves. Jesus, her phone had over five calls from a blocked number. Someone was trying to reach her. She thought of calling Ray Infantino. But she didn't make the call. She didn't want to speak with anyone right now.

Somewhere far off, she heard a basketball pounding on the pavement. She peeked from behind shades into the gathering dusk, the once-familiar street a black vein running into a dangerous tomorrow. Then she sat down and let the smoke lead her into oblivion.

CHAPTER 32

McBAIN TOOK AIM and fired several rounds from the Smith & Wesson .44 revolver. Bullets smashed into a stand of slender birches, and the trunks just evaporated into a matchstick storm of wet pulp and bark. The tree tops tumbled off kilter to the ground. Jake Noonan's backyard now looked like a strange graveyard of stub three-foot tree trunks.

Noonan had a good thing here in this zero-stop-light town, some forty miles west of Boston. A bit of wild west mentality out here. You could shoot out targets on private property if you were five hundred feet away from a dwelling. Take that, red staters. Ol' Massachusetts, blue as blue could be, still paid some respect to the revolutionary spirit that founded this great nation. He'd bring his son out here when he had him next weekend. That was the problem with the younger generation. People forgot that there was nothing wrong with a show of force and imposing your will in a physical way. He grew up taking beatings from his father in the 1970s. He just wanted to pass down the lesson.

"You want to see something special?" Noonan wore that grin that saw him still tossing smoke bombs into restaurant bathrooms. Old jesters never die. Noonan reached over to a bag sitting on a rough-hewn table he kept outside and pulled out a compact revolver, a single-shot derringer. "Picked it up last week at a gun show in New Haven." He took a little hop over and handed it to McBain. "Try it."

McBain chuckled as he handled it. The weapon was no bigger than a cell phone. He aimed and fired into the target. The accuracy of such a little weapon surprised him. The gun fit Noonan: a clever piece for a clever little bastard.

McBain and Noonan came up together in Southie during the 1970s. There was an incident they both still spoke about occasionally, a little touchstone of old-school education that welded the friendship forever. They were walking to a bus stop that day like so many kids did. But it was no ordinary day. Buses were rolling in, filled with Black kids from city neighborhoods like Jamaica Plain and Roxbury. And McBain was shipping out. A federal judge had ruled that the funding of Boston schools was unequal and that the solution was to integrate all schools by forced busing. So, even if a student was content with a neighborhood school, whether it be in Roxbury or Southie, they were getting on a bus to go somewhere else the next morning. The forced integration of the schools in Boston painted Boston as a racist city, an image that lasted for decades.

Like other poor kids from Southie, McBain had no say in being shipped to Jamaica Plain, where they had their own integration problems. His first day there, he watched a group of Black students, roiled by news stories about the vitriol directed at Black kids being bussed to South Boston, look for some getback. Ten Black kids surrounded a white kid on the playground. The white kid was Jake Noonan, a scrawny brainiac who McBain knew from the neighborhood school. Surrounded by a twenty-legged mob, Noonan was writhing in pain on the ground as they kicked and punched him. McBain saw Noonan hurt and waded into the crowd, swinging a jagged piece of wood. He sliced one kid across the face and laid into the rest with a frightening vigor, skewering boys and girls alike until he fell beneath a tide of kids stomping on him. McBain damaged his knee, and from that day on, he walked with a hitch in his gait. Noonan lost a kidney after that beating. But from that day on, Noonan was a blood brother.

A bitterness spread inside McBain. Only he and Noonan took the bus ride over from their street. His father was dead; his mother worked two jobs. For the entire school year, he dealt with it, fighting almost daily with the Black kids, usually two on one or worse. McBain made sure he got his retaliation in first. They expelled him several times. And there was always another kid to fight when he returned.

They were a lost generation, those kids from 1974. The schools turned more dangerous than the streets, and when you got back to your neighborhood, more trouble awaited at home. One of his best friends dropped out of school, forced by his parents to defy the court order in the only way they knew how. They gutted their children's education to spite the federal decree. Adults who should have known better dissolved into mindless diatribes against the city and spit venom on Black people, the only people poorer than they were. Men who worked the underworld saw the new recruits on the streets. Dozens of kids like him, White and Black, graduated into a different, less liberal kind of education where lessons were dealt out on the docks, in barrooms on Broadway, on leafy sidewalks in Franklin Park. In the end, the only winners were the gangs.

McBain kept the humiliation of those days close to his heart. The scars over his eyebrows were just an outward sign of the damage. Down inside, something vital scabbed over. He vowed no man would ever tell him what side of the street he could walk on. From that day, he would tread wherever he wished. Any screwball who questioned that right would get a baseball bat slammed off their skull. He even got on the police force for a few years and donned the blue as a one-man revenge machine. When he lost that job after working over a suspect in an alleyway, he went back to the streets. Men who could kick ass could always find a spot in police forces or gangs.

And now here they were, decades removed from the buses and the projects, just two good Southie boys shooting at birch trees in a rural backyard.

They fired off some more rounds and then headed back to the house for a few beers. Noonan put the Red Sox game on the TV.

"So, that thing we discussed. What do you have so far?" asked McBain.

"The North End is bringing up coke from Providence by using produce deliveries at some warehouse on the North Shore."

"I need to know where. I need truck owners' names and when they come."

"No problem, I'll make some calls," said Noonan, who worked for a trucking company that shipped to several outlets at the Chelsea Depot. If anyone knew about secret deliveries, Noonan would get word.

"The laundry is being done at a bakery in the North End. Taormina."

"How do you know?"

Noonan laughed. "This driver does the drop and he fuckin' loves the place. He comes out with a bag of treats every time. The name Taormina is right on the bag!"

McBain had to laugh. Noonan went into the other room to make some calls about the trucking.

* * *

Later that evening, McBain drove back on the Mass Pike into Boston. He pulled off in Back Bay, whipped around the Copley Square hotels, and headed to the Common. Around 9 p.m., he parked near the Piano Row District on Tremont and grabbed a coffee from a cafe. He walked over to the ball fields where the lights stayed on late and some guys were taking turns hitting. His contact was sitting there already, which irritated him. He preferred to get to meetings first and wait. This appealed to his sense of hunting. He sat down and sipped his coffee.

"Nice night," said Baden, a tall, wiry man with burned-out eyes set deep in a chiseled face that reminded McBain of a crow. But Baden was okay for a state trooper.

"Beautiful. How's the family?"

"Girls are doing well in school. All you can ask for. How's your boy?"

McBain grunted. "I got him on the weekends. Good kid. Miracle, considering."

They watched one guy smash a ball toward Charles Street.

"What's happening in Providence?"

"Taormina Bakery launders the powder money. These are some guys we looked at." He gave some names and numbers to Baden. "Plate numbers are the trucks they run product with to Boston, Manchester and the west, Albany, and up to Vermont. Then back to the bakery with the cash."

"Looks good. Actionable."

No shit, Sherlock. thought McBain. *We tell you*

who to arrest. Do it like dumb little foot soldiers in our blue army.

"And the guys working with you?" asked Baden.

"Same guys. Same areas. No problems so far."

Baden seemed to mull something over. They watched a bit more of the game. Baden turned to him. "This has been a hot summer so far. They fished another body out of the harbor last week."

"Yeah, I saw the news."

"Bill Hagstrom, a dealer. He took two shots in the head and one in the mouth. Any ideas?"

McBain looked blank and shook his head. "No idea. We don't know this guy at all."

A fight broke out at second base; the throw was late, and the runner sideswiped the shortstop coming over to cover. People took photos with their cell phones. Brawling on the posh side of town. Baden was looking at McBain again.

"Information we have, he was bragging at a bar downtown that he refused to pay rent to South Boston. He had his own crew."

"This guy was not known to us. Small time. What's his name again, Hagstrom?"

Baden frowned. "Come on, Tommy. No one is too small for a shakedown."

Tommy nodded. "Of course. But we're not crazy." The specter of a smile crept across his face, dead before it arrived.

Baden nodded and looked away, shaking his

head. "Keep in mind that the office will not sanction this stuff. Street hits will be fully investigated."

"Of course. You were clear on that."

"But the bakery informant—"

"That's what you want, right? The North End boys get you paid." McBain knew this guy was already jacking off with the tip on the Mafia. No one in the FBI or state police got intel like this, direct from a source. The spigot was running and McBain could puppet these troopers for years.

Baden glared at him and then looked away. They watched the ball game. McBain didn't want to leave on an unpleasant note, so he made agreeable sounds in the trooper's direction. Then he walked off into the Common while Baden stared after him.

CHAPTER 33

BUTTERS SAT IN his apartment and called the number again. No answer. He sat back, sipped his beer, and waited for the call back. The phone rang, and he picked up.

"Who's this."

"Joe Butters."

"Where did you get this number?"

"A friend. McBain."

Pause. "Here's the deal. You're going to a party. There's a guy, a client and his wife, swingers. She likes it rough. Nipple clamps, getting choked a little, all that shit. So she wants to do this role-play thing where she's tied up and gets fucked by a couple of anonymous guys. It's set up at a place on Revere Beach. So you come in and she pretends she doesn't want it. But she does. This guy, he's a good client. So we want to accommodate."

Butters listened. It sounded weird. "So, I just show up?"

"Yeah. You'll get five low on this. Best work you can get. We're paying you to screw, my friend." The man laughed. "Check in with me tomorrow."

"So she knows I'm coming?"

"Yeah."

"Okay," said Butters slowly.

"This is a role-play situation. You just go there and be yourself. Spank her butt, whatever she wants. This is what this couple pays for. All that bond-age shit."

"Right."

"Good people, good clients. See you tomorrow after showtime."

The call ended.

CHAPTER 34

RAY PUNCHED AUGUSTINA'S number into his cell again. No answer. A few days ago, he took a call from Augustina and she went off like a bomb, demanding to know if he had sent someone to watch her—there was a guy walking up and down the sidewalk, and strange cars prowling the street.

He explained that those were not his people, and offered to set up surveillance at her place to make sure she was okay. She hung up before he could finish.

He had gone to see her several times, but she was out or not answering. Maybe paranoia was getting the best of Augustina. Ray was troubled. He sent one of his best guys, Aaron Roth, to watch her house. Roth sat out there all day but saw nothing unusual. Roth also made periodic checks at Butters' place in the North End to keep tabs on him. Butters was nowhere to be seen.

Ray headed over to the back fields near Harvard Stadium to meet Marquez for football practice. The men wore practice gear with the blue and white of the Boston Midnight Riders. The team played in a flag football league but that did not prevent certain players from tattooing a helmet imprint onto a quarterback or blasting an iron shoulder into an opponent's ribs. They could creatively execute these maneuvers within the rules. Penalty flags were only a suggestion.

Marquez played middle linebacker and several players were growing irritated by his karate chops on their forearms. A wide receiver shoved Marquez after a play. Marquez just laughed at him.

"This is what they're going to do to you on Sunday."

"Take it easy Marquez!"

Marquez shook his head in disgust. "He keeps running into my momentum." Marquez's shoulders looked like they came from some loping creature from a distant era, just raw power. He was known for de-cleating opponents, lowering a shoulder and sending them hurtling through the air. What he lacked in speed, he made up for in brutality. He led the league in penalties. Marquez thought it was good to be a league leader in something.

Ray took some snaps as the quarterback. According to Marquez, this made him the most over-paid player—based on minutes played—on the team. Ray ran some power sweeps with Marquez swooping in for late hits, laughing at Ray each time he reached him. They loved this game. The simple camaraderie of sports, a group working toward a common goal.

They moved to the passing drills. After practicing some basic wheel routes and slants, Ray faded back and threw a long spiral out to the receiver, who beat the cornerback with the old dead-leg move. Then they ran the same play. But this time Marquez bull-rushed the lineman, Peter O'Brien, who stumbled back as Marquez ran over him. O'Brien reached up and pulled him down by the groin. As Marquez fell, he tenderized O'Brien's stomach with a knee smash. O'Brien lay on the ground and gasped for breath.

"That was holding!" Marquez shouted.

O'Brien got up and shoved Marquez, and a brawl broke out. The pork chop head of the line coach intervened. "Marquez! I need live players on Sunday!" But the coach looked happy. He was a veteran coach who played college ball down south, where they restricted water breaks and believed that a good brawl was a sign of team bonding.

Ray was showering after practice when a call came in from Roth.

"Augustina was home after all. She left in a hurry in a taxi. We followed her from her place to an apartment on Revere Beach. She went up an hour ago. Not coming back down. But you wouldn't believe who just walked into the building. The guy from the North End, Butters."

Ray dressed quickly, took his Beretta 9mm pistol out of a locker in his trunk, and raced away from the field.

CHAPTER 35

AFTER THE SCARE with the car staking out her house, Augustina kept a low profile. But she needed to work. The next day she went out the back way and dialed a car service to pick her up at the corner. She got to work at the Golden Banana before noon.

There was a line of guys at the free buffet, which consisted of chicken wings from last night, oily french fries, and sliders made of some sauce mixed with beef. There was not a vegetable within a hundred miles of the place.

Her first dance was scheduled in an hour so she went to the bar for a ginger ale. She was working as "Nikki" now, and Nikki was in need of some cash for the week. Bills were piling up on her desk at home—her kids' medical bills, tuition bills, the usual utilities. It was tough, but she promised herself she would finish school this time.

She saw one of her regulars, Michael, sitting at a table. His feet were popping off the floor in rhythm to "Girls Girls Girls" by Motley Crue. 1980s rock still played well with the clients. Michael had been in for lunch a few times over the last few months. Not a bad-looking guy, Irish tinge to his face, one of these quarterback-types back in the day. He worked in the construction business, he told her. He was her lunchtime ATM that week, pushing twenty-dollar bills into her G-string like they burned his fingers. She liked real men, old-fashioned gents who knew a girl could spin the fantasy better without paying too much attention to where the cash was going.

"Hey Nikki, how are you?"

She gave him a peck on the cheek and sat down, letting her leg brush against him. "Working hard, baby?"

"Sure. Dead in here today," he said.

They talked for a while and watched the next dancer, Capri, shimmy up and down the pole like a brown panther, a tattoo on her back of a cat and an arrow pointing south that said, "Kiss my kitty." Capri said that she got it last year on a murky weekend in Providence. Augustina wasn't sure what to say; the tattoo was hideous.

"Hey, listen," Michael said, sipping his beer, "Do you ever see clients outside? You know, private shows?"

"Not really. Just in here, hon. I don't know you."

"Well, we've been friends since last week's buffet."

She laughed at that.

"Well, if you change your mind. I'm thinking five hundred. I like to relax."

She went off to use the bathroom. The club

warned the girls about seeing clients outside the bar, but five hundred per hour was sweet and Michael seemed alright. He had been in here a half-dozen times at least, and the bartenders knew him.

She wasn't supposed to do it, but she planned to meet him the next day at his place in Revere.

The next afternoon, Augustina went out the back way again and tapped her phone for a car. Michael's apartment was on a busy stretch of Revere Beach, which made her feel good. Revere Beach was one of the oldest public beaches in America. The city had cleaned the place up, straightened out the parking situation, and still had North Shore characters walking all over the place. It kept an urban feel, lots of Brazilians at one end, older Italians still claiming rights to spots here and there. There was the usual line at Kelly's Roast Beef and the smell of pizza slices from Bianchi's.

She told the driver to drop her off a little ways down from the address. His place was a hulking pink stucco apartment building that squatted like a Sphinx over the boardwalk. She texted him she was down the street. He texted her back to come on up.

She moved into the hallway to apartment four. When she got there, she knocked, and the door opened. It was Michael. She stepped inside. Then his face disappeared as something came down over her head. She screamed as something jammed into her mouth that tasted acidic. In the half light, she felt herself tossed down to the floor by rough hands and then faded to gray silence.

CHAPTER 36

BUTTERS TOOK A taxi over to Revere Beach Boulevard and gazed across the street for the right address. An old guy sat in a lawn chair across by the seawall, his chest brown as a leather hide. He was setting a friend straight. "They think they know shit. But they don't know shit. That's the problem with my kids." The friend nodded and glanced over at two young women prancing by in neon green exercise bras.

Butters sighed. He had fond memories of chasing tanned beauties here in his youth. Easier days, that's what he wanted. Wouldn't mind a chance to sit out in the sun like those old buzzards and do nothing. But wolves were at the door and he wouldn't sniff retirement for another two decades.

He got to the address of the beachside complex, a garish pink high-rise, and rang the apartment. The buzzer went off and he entered the hallway. Clean and white, devoid of any details. The apartment was on the fifth floor. He rang but heard nothing. Then the lock slid back, and the door opened. He stepped inside a darkened room. A dark-haired man in a white shirt and jeans stood there, pointed to a back bedroom, and said he would let himself out. Butters nodded. He walked to the bedroom.

When his eyes adjusted to the dimness, he saw a woman, bound and gagged, lying on her side. She had long, dark hair that fell across her face. She was dressed in light green lingerie. Her left nipple was peeking out over her bra.

Butters was surprised. He had expected some chubby chick who was into this kind of kink. The woman was beautiful. She shook her head frantically.

This was the client. Time to start the show.

He removed his shirt and sat on the bed, then kicked off his boots with a thud. The woman was struggling now, lifting her arms up in jerky movements that caused the duct tape to bore into her skin. God, these crazed middle-class housewives were so bored they did nothing but fantasize about rough sex.

He stood ready to get naked. Then he looked at the woman's face again, more closely this time. Something went slack in his chest. This girl's eyes, her entire face, radiated fear. He could see it. It was a look he had seen before. The face of a kid getting a gang beat down in the alleys off Dot Ave when he was a kid. He saw it once when a kid named Johnny Wheeler took a bullet and bled out on a courtyard in the projects.

If this girl was acting, then she was the best in the

business. The whole thing smelled bad. He thought back to McBain bumping into him that day after the visit to probation, and the phone call to the voice on the phone. He reached over and got ready to pull off her gag. Then he stopped.

"They told me this was something you wanted. A fantasy thing." The girl shook her head no, no, no, no. "Who set this up? Do you know?" She shook her head no again, a small sliver of relief crossing her cheekbones.

"Damn!" He sat back. Then he reached down and pulled on his boots and shirt. He waited for five minutes, thinking over every possibility while the woman with the beautiful black hair just stared at him without making a sound. "I, ah...never knew this was what they were doing."

He pulled off her gag, and she drew in oxygen in a ragged gulp. "Oh God, oh God! Thank you, they did this! Some guy set this up!"

"Who?"

She hesitated. "Michael. I don't know his real name."

"Well, neither do I."

Butters took out a pocket knife, and the woman looked at him with dread in her eyes. He shook his head. "The tape." She raised her wrists. He snipped the tape, making sure not to cut her. Then he moved to her legs. Soon she was free. She stood up and stared at him as if looking for guidance on what to do next.

Butters looked at her. "Lady, whatever reason you're here, you gotta make it out yourself. I'm a dead man now." Then Butters got up and left the room.

CHAPTER 37

RAY ROARED UP the boulevard on Revere Beach. The sidewalks were crowded with people enjoying the beach: old men strolling, young mothers with kids, girls in bright bikinis. He noticed a dark-haired woman wearing a dress pop out from a side alley and hurry south on the boardwalk. It was Augustina. There was no place to pull over, so he drove another twenty feet and then skidded to a stop in front of a pavilion. He called Roth.

"Where are you?" Ray asked.

"I'm in front of the apartment. Butters left in a hurry and grabbed a cab. I stayed here in case Augustina came out."

"Good. I just saw her now, coming out a side door and heading south."

Ray hung up and began jogging south on the beachside boulevard. He could see Augustina ahead. She hurried down the sidewalk and scanned left to right nervously, rubbing her wrists. Ray called out to her.

Augustina looked startled. Then she recognized him. For half a second, she looked like she was ready to run. She leaned against a car and buried her face in her hands. Ray jogged up to her and stopped to catch his breath.

"Augustina, what happened—"

"They're after me!"

"I had a guy out at your house after what you told me. We were worried—"

"I should have told you. I was…" She groped for words. Her brow was furrowed, and she struggled to continue. "These people, my God, they will do anything to stop me. I feel sick."

"What happened?"

She said nothing, just stared back toward a pink high-rise building. Ray followed her gaze and saw two men step outside the building where she had just come from. They seemed to look down the street at them. The men were talking and gesturing down the boulevard, but they did not approach.

"You know them?"

She looked over. "God, no."

Ray stared at the men. Maybe it was nothing. Augustina sat back and sighed. He leaned on the car.

"What happened in there?"

"There was a guy at the club. Seemed nice, had the money. Asked me for private dances. I know, I know, it was stupid. I came to that apartment build-ing." She pointed to the cement hulk a block away. "I texted him. And when I came into the room, I saw his face for a second. He was there, and then he was gone. They put something over my mouth. I really don't remember. My head is killing me."

"They drugged you."

Her head lolled, and she closed her eyes against the pain splintering her forehead. "I woke up, couldn't move. My hands were taped together. Then after a while, a man walked in the room. He seemed to think I was part of a scene, like an S&M set up. I was trying to tell him no." She shook her head.

"Did he—"

"No, thank God. He could tell I was freaking out. He asked me if I knew who did this and then he left. Said something about being a dead man."

"I know this guy." It stunned Ray that the South Boston crew had gone to such an extreme measure to get Butters and Augustina together in a room. Intimidation, a warning to both of them, a way to destroy both of them as witnesses. Amazingly, Butters had done the right thing and walked out.

"Is he the police?" Augustina asked.

Ray looked at her. "Him? No. But he was a witness in the same case."

She shook her head in disbelief.

"Yes." Ray looked down the beach at the gathering crowd at the pavilion. "And now, they're gunning for him."

CHAPTER 38

THEY GOT IN Ray's car and Augustina tried to get her bearings. Ray stared back at the apartment building. There was no one outside. He leaned out the window and pulled away into traffic.

"You should file a report with the Revere police. Let them investigate who rents the apartment, the guy who approached you at the strip club. I'll work on it too, but I want as much pressure on these guys as possible."

She nodded, looking numb. Ray suspected the arrows pointed to the Electric House crew in South Boston. A sense of foreboding clouded his mind, unseen dangers looming just over the horizon. Setting up Augustina to be raped in an apartment showed that Magnus and his ilk would take any measure to make sure the old crime remained pinned on Langford. He felt terrible that Augustina was caught in the middle and mauled by larger forces.

Ray drove her to the police station. She said very

little to the detectives; she didn't seem to trust them, even though this was a different police department than Boston's. After they finished the interview, he took her back to her apartment. He walked her inside. She looked haggard.

"Thanks, Ray. I need to be left alone."

"I could have one of my guys come over, keep an eye on the place."

She nodded without really hearing. Ray would take no chances with her. He put in a call to Roth and told him to make it over to her place as soon as he could. Roth arrived, Ray briefed him on the plan, and then Ray took off.

The tunnel back to the city was jammed, so he drove through the city of Chelsea toward the waterfront. He turned right on a potholed street where the midnight trucks pulled into the cargo docks at the massive produce warehouses that serviced the New England states. The place thrummed in the early morning but now it was quiet. He stopped for a coffee. Some off-duty truckers were heading to a seedy strip joint where Brazilian strippers spoke no English but communicated in a more primitive tongue with men at the bar.

He took a shortcut through the deserted warehouse district to the Chelsea Bridge. As he drove down a battered road, a police cruiser came up from behind, the blue Christmas lights twinkling in the mirror. He sighed and pulled over.

The cruiser pulled behind him. No one exited.

He was parked on a dim stretch of road and couldn't see whether the cop had gotten out of the cruiser yet. Then he saw two doors open. Two police officers, silhouettes in a spectral haze. He rolled down the windows, warm air rushing in. One cop was a strapping guy, with a mid-hip bulge of cuffs and gun. His partner hung back on the other side.

Ray strained to see details in the shadows. To the right, a truck rolled by, rattling over the cracked asphalt. The two shadows separated, one man hanging behind, one approaching the window with his arm held stiffly at his side. A brief glint of headlights from the truck back-lit the cops before the blackness fell. Ray saw the cops were wearing jeans and sneakers.

These were no cops.

He turned the ignition and peeled away.

"Hey, what the fuck?" one man shouted. He raised a gun but fired no shots. Ray saw the two men race back to the car.

Ray roared down the broken street past a steel fence running along a salvage yard. The siren lights behind him dimmed. He dialed 911.

"What is your emergency?"

"Someone impersonating cops in Chelsea. They just pulled me over near the produce center. One guy had a gun."

"Do you have a description?"

"Driving a Crown Vic or something like it."

"Where are you now?"

"Driving on Beacham."

"Are you hurt?"

"Just my feelings."

"What?"

"I'm okay."

"Stay on the line, please."

He saw lights flash in the rearview and dropped the phone in his shirt pocket. He crossed a rutted road that ran under the iron towers of the Tobin Bridge, where traffic from the city of Boston passed over the harbor. Metal shimmered at the edges of his periphery. Corners of brick buildings, a sidewalk, people waking. No way they would try something here.

Then behind him, blinding light filled the horizon like an earthbound star. A crack-crack-crack of gunshots close by. He could see a car behind him, the window down, some activity in the window frame. A sense of sudden motion on the sidewalk, people running all over the place in silent pantomimes of panic.

The car stayed behind him. He could see a disembodied hand in the half light aiming at him out the window. The hand was bobbing and jerking, whether because of the rough road or adrenaline overrunning the sluices, he could not say. The shots missed the mark.

He reached and pulled the Beretta from his holster. He pushed the pedal on a curve, drew away, and then slowed down. Then he turned, gun in hand. The dark shape of the car was just behind him on the turn. He drew his attention to smudging out the shape with the tip of the gun barrel. Then he fired. Not panicked, just a calculated breathe and squeeze drill. Get lead in front of their faces. Get 'em dead.

The dark car shuddered and veered off to the right, smashed into a cement wall, then skidded to a halt in front of an empty lot twenty yards away. He saw the driver's body slouched over the steering wheel. That was good. But he couldn't see the other guy.

Ray leapt out of his car and ran behind a cement wall. No more running; too great a chance of an accident, or unlucky shots hitting him. He wanted to attack.

He scanned the dark lot behind the car. Then the car moved almost imperceptibly, weight shifting. He heard the passenger door fly open and something fell to the ground. Someone was out, crouched behind the far side passenger door.

Two tractor trailers stopped on the street. The drivers were watching the gunfight near the iron ramparts like it was a Bruins game. This apparently was a human need. It defied the instinct of self-preservation, but people just had to watch the damn thing.

Ray crouched down and peered underneath the car frame. One trucker fired up his high beams and the barren lot lit up like a carnival of decay: trash-strewn pavement, crumbling brick walls, old tires. A man-shaped shadow bloomed on the brick wall—the man was moving.

Ray fired off three shots at the car and burst a

tire, a rattle of metal on metal. Then the rat-a-tat dance of feet on asphalt. The misty white tubes of light from the trucks riddled the night. Glass shards on the pavement glittered in a silver constellation. He could see the guy now, running into the weeds near the harbor. He held something in his right hand.

Ray jogged behind him, keeping to the shadows. He knew he should let it go; the police were on their way. But there was something in his blood now, he couldn't stop it. The instinct to fight trumped his common sense. He was raging.

He could see that the guy in front of him was heavyset and starting to tire. There was something herky-jerky about his movements. Off to one side, he could hear the rubbery buzz of tires crossing the metal bridge.

Then he heard a soft splash. He looked out to the harbor, a smudge of roiling gray on black. The waves were slight here. He could hear a light splashing as someone paddled in the dark sea with little finesse and more than a tinge of panic. No way to see who it was.

Ray felt energized but strangely calm, surfing the peak of a primal rush, eyes raking the water for a target. He took a deep breath. There, to the right, sounds of splashing and then a shape materialized. Yes, he could see the silhouette now, clambering up the rocks below the bridge.

Ray jogged across a small footbridge, traffic lights blazing yellow. As Ray got to the other side, he heard the man's heavy breathing from the rocks below. Ray went down under the bridge, stationed himself at the top of the rocks, and drew his gun.

"You move, you die, fatfuck."

The guy had dark hair and a fighter's ruined face, all scars and crevices. He was panting, out of shape and gassed from the swim. Blood ran down his leg from a wound.

"Put your hands up behind your head," Ray yelled down. This was all he knew. He had never been a cop, never arrested someone. But he suspected this guy had done a few live rehearsals before. He kept to the high ground and trained the gun on the man's chest.

He took out his phone left-handed and re-dialed 911. The operator took the information and told him there were dozens of calls about this incident.

"Maybe so," he said. "But I have the shooter at gunpoint." That kept her interest, and she told him to stay on the line. He thought for a moment and then hung up.

The guy looked at him. "Can I sit down?"

"No."

"Okay."

"Who are you working for?" Ray asked.

"No one."

"Why me?"

"Just convenience."

Ray had to laugh. "Convenience?" He stepped down to the rocks and the guy's eyes got real wide. "Take out your wallet."

"I don't have it."

Ray pointed to a bulge in the man's front-right pocket. "Take it out. Or I'll put a hole in your other leg."

The guy sighed and then reached down with one hand, pulled out his wallet, and held it in his hand.

"Toss it over to me." The guy tossed it, wincing at the effort.

Ray caught it, opened it up, and pulled out the guy's license. Luis Pereira of East Boston. Ray took out his phone and, still holding the gun on Pereira, placed the license on a large rock that came up to his waist. Then he snapped a picture of the license. Ray could hear voices from an unseen group of people moving along the bridge. Sirens cried in the distance. But Ray and Pereira remained out of sight under the bridge.

Ray kept the gun trained on Pereira, but thought he would try a different tactic. "You like steak? We should talk over a meal."

Pereira looked confused.

"I'm serious. Why does it have to end like this?" Ray said. "I just want to talk with you."

The guy smiled in genuine relief that he would not get shot in the nuts after all. "Yeah, okay."

"Who sent you?"

"Come on, man."

"Who?"

"A number, that was all I know."

"Toss me your cell phone."

Pereira reached down into his pocket and pulled out a cell phone. He tossed it to Ray, who caught it with his free hand and put it on the rock next to the license. A cheap burner phone. There were four numbers in the call log, three of them from tonight.

Ray snapped a photo of the call log with his own cell phone. Then they waited for the sirens to get closer.

Pereira was still breathing hard. "Listen man, this wasn't anything personal. Can't play it that way." He laughed a little and shrugged his shoulders like it was all part of a game.

"I'd feel better if it was," said Ray, his voice low with malice. He took a step toward Pereira and gazed down at him. Pereira shook his head as if trying to work out the meaning.

Ray felt a jolt of fury. The crime game, where the less you know, the better you sleep. It was always someone else's fault. This guy was the same as Bobby Cherry, who murdered his fiancée years ago in San Francisco. Just like any criminal who stooped to mindless violence for a few coins. Acts of violence in the anonymous dark, that was how they survived.

Ray listened to the plaintive cry of the sirens. The sound was piercing. He stood still for a second longer, knowing he shouldn't do it, but couldn't stop the venom flowing—he stepped in and kicked Pereira in the stomach. Pereira went flying off the rocks and slipped into a crevice near the waterline. Ray felt the fury burn through his limbs. He stalked over and aimed another kick at Pereira, catching him in the leg, the inside meat of the thigh. Pereira grunted and seemed resigned to the beating, pulling himself up on the rocks. Ray stomped on a hand splayed on the rock and heard a bone crack. Pereira screamed in pain.

Ray caught himself and stopped, caught his breath. Pereira groaned as he crawled back to the rock and slumped over his ruined hand. Then a police prowl car arrived on the street. A minute later, two cops peered over the edge of the bridge. Young guys, both fit and alert. They looked down at Ray and Pereira.

"Did you make the call?"

"Yes, I did. This guy's ID is on the rock there."

"Hope you got a permit for that thing," the cop said.

"I do," Ray said. The cops stepped down to the rocks. Ray handed over his driver's license and fire-arms ID card to one of them. Pereira was moaning and holding his left wrist.

"What happened to him?" one policeman asked.

"He slipped."

"Yeah, they usually do."

"He kicked me," Pereira muttered.

"Lucky. He could have shot you."

"I thought of that," Ray said.

The other cop stepped over the rocks to handcuff Pereira. Voices from the bridge above filtered over the water. Traffic stalled at the intersection, the spot-lights speckling the bridge with yellow. Ray knew it would be a long night before he got home.

CHAPTER 39

IT WAS PAST midnight when Butters slid down a side street and walked toward his apartment building. He slowed beneath a tree a block down from his home and peered over at the house. No lights on, shades drawn, front door looked closed, just as he had left it.

Still, he had a bad feeling after today's debacle.

For years, McBain had pawned him off for all the dirty jobs that needed to be done. The work was nasty, but the woman in the Revere Beach apartment was the final straw. He wasn't sure who she was, or why she was there, but that was a staged scene, he knew it. When he went inside the apartment, she looked so beautiful it seemed like a dream job. Play with her a bit and then take her every way a man could think. That was what she paid for, the voice on the phone had told him. But her struggle with her bindings was too real, her fear convinced him, and when she looked up at him, he saw it at last. He was being played again.

The question was why McBain was doing this to him now. It all related to that private investigator digging into the old business at the waterfront. When McBain discovered Butters had left the place without doing the job on the witness, well, that was the end of his freedom in the city.

Looking around again, he trudged across the silent street. A light rain came down in a soft patter on the pavement. No one stepped out of a car, no one hassled him. God, he just wanted to get back home. He stepped up to his doorway.

"Mr. Butters." He whipped around. The private detective who had come at him a while ago, Ray Infantino, stood on the sidewalk.

"You guys ever call?"

"I know what happened in Revere. They came after me, too. Let's talk for a few minutes."

Butters sighed, pushed open the door, and walked inside the hallway. They went upstairs and entered the apartment. The rooms smelled stale, beer bottles stacked on a coffee table, little green soldiers laying siege to an empty pizza box. They sat down on the sofa.

"So you followed me here?"

"No." Ray saw Butters frown. "We were watching her."

"Why?"

"She was worried that she was being targeted."

"Who is she?"

"She testified in the same case you did."

Butters' face went still.

"I think I warned you this was not going away."

"Yeah, you did. You want a beer?" asked Butters. "I'm gonna get a beer."

"No, thanks."

Butters went to the kitchen and came back with a bottle of Miller.

"So, what happened at the beach apartment?"

Butters said nothing for a long time, just staring at his beer bottle. "I was told that there would be a woman in that apartment. That I was to go to the apartment, be part of this rough sex scene. People pay for this stuff."

"But who told you about this?"

Butters hesitated. Ray let him wallow in the silence for a bit. "I don't know the guy."

"How did you get the location?"

"Phone call."

"Did you recognize this girl?"

"No. Never seen her in my life. Pretty, though."

"Both of you testified on this Sam Langford case. And now, over a decade and a half later, you end up in the same room together. Someone has a warped idea of intimidation."

"Holy shit." Butters sat there and looked down at his feet.

"Why didn't you go through with it?"

Butters shook his head. He had never harmed women in his jobs and he was not about to start. "That's not me."

"They set you both up."

Butters stared at him. "I know."

Ray got up and looked out the window. A few late-night diners were walking from the restaurants on Hanover Street. He turned back to Butters. "Sam Langford's been away for a long time. Isn't it time to just let the truth come out on this case?"

Butters stared at Ray for a few heartbeats. But he said nothing.

"We can help you. It doesn't have to end like this."

Butters stirred at this and rubbed his forehead. He couldn't go there with this investigator, there was too much on the line. "Look, I appreciate what you are trying to do. I'm sorry for the guy. But I can't talk to you no more."

"Look man, whatever instinct made you stop when you saw that woman, don't snuff it out."

Butters snorted. "Won't matter. After today, I'm like that movie. Dead man walking."

CHAPTER 40

RAY WOKE EARLY the next morning and went for a jog through the city, trying to pound out his frustration from the events of the previous night. He felt better when he was done. He showered and dressed in a linen shirt with dark dress pants and loafers. Ray walked a few blocks over to Shawmut to meet Tania at a cafe and took a seat outside. The cafe had the kind of hard metal chairs that ensured no one could overstay their welcome.

Tania arrived a few minutes later, wearing jeans and a white cotton shirt that set off her California tan. A waitress brought coffee to the table. Ray and Tania sat and talked while the young, and young at heart, danced their elaborate courting rituals on the narrow brick sidewalks. A late summer sun shot autumn crocuses from the earth, the air scented with an earthy scent that made sinews pulsate with life. Ray rubbed his shoulder. Football practice had re-aggravated an old skiing injury. He felt a twinge as he rotated it. The battle against aging was not much of a battle when the opposing side had overwhelming numbers.

Before the meeting, he had checked the numbers he pulled off the cell phone logs from the fake cop Pereira, but nothing came of it as the numbers were all burner phones. The name of the dead driver was still being determined by police; his license turned out to be fake. So it was time to focus again on Davin Price.

"You did well getting inside the group in San Diego. Now I need the same focus on this guy Price in the Southie crew."

"Thank you. You taught me well."

"True. But you're going to be better than me."

She looked surprised by the comment.

"It's true. People open up to you. I can see it. You have a gift."

She shifted her body as if uncomfortable with the compliment. "I love this work. You gave me a chance when I was down."

Tania sat back and Ray looked over at her again, that chiseled forehead over her unreadable eyes, an inscrutable wall that kept the world at bay at all times. It must be interesting to look at the world through a face like that. A face that made people want to please her, to do things for her. Then again, it did not help her avoid predators in her own family when they stripped her of everything she had before her father's ashes grew cold. The curious blessings of life: A fabulous face attracted ill will as often as it did admiring glances.

They were equals now. Time for the falcon to fly. But it meant a closing of sorts, an ending to what had come before. He felt a melancholy plume run through his belly. It was strange, this sensation of mingled sadness and joy, a gust riding below a summer day. He didn't want her to see him like this, getting nostalgic. He looked away and focused on people in the street.

"So on Sam Langford's appeal, we have three witnesses: Joey Butters, Davin Price, Augustina Calderon. Price blew me off early in the investigation. So I have been working on Butters and Augustina. Making progress until last week." He described how someone had conspired to intimidate the two witnesses, or at least cloud the waters. "I think they came up with a simple plan. A message was intended for both of them: Unpleasant things will follow if they become too involved in this case."

Tania shook her head in disgust. "Sick people."

"That is the way with these things. In a world of wolves and sheep, they want these two to remember their roles. These two are insignificant flecks on the horizon. And by shutting their mouths, they could remain that way."

"But now Butters might start to believe otherwise."

"Maybe," said Ray. "But I was not encouraged after my talk with him last night. So I want to return to Price. I saw him once before but this is where you come in. He was a longtime informant for the police. We need to know more about his role."

They went over the research on Price: He had gone into the underworld like his father, and learned to provide outlets for the foibles of man. This was Price's racket, the shadow economy that ran on its own rules, had its own bankers. The bankers charged interest. If you didn't pay on time, you paid on the loan in a different way. A guy like Price stopped by your home and played a drum solo on your knee-cap with a hammer. The efficiency of the underworld marketplace meant you didn't need police because everyone had their own, small militias who settled beefs during evening appointments in the backseats of cars or inside paint-peeling warehouses.

The waitress brought the bill as Ray and Tania finished their coffees. Outside, he wished her good luck. "You're great in these situations. You will get what we need. I believe it."

Tania reached out and hugged him. Ray lingered for a moment, not sure of what to do. Then, without a word, they went their separate ways outside the cafe.

CHAPTER 41

TANIA WALKED A few blocks before hailing a ride to South Boston. She got out on Broadway and entered a door below a sign with a cool blue neon rocket rising into the air: the Moonshot Diner. She noticed Davin Price, commandeering the diner with a salty braggadocio. Tania sat down at a table near Price.

The surveillance team had been on him for a few days. Price came here regularly, cruising around Broadway, stopping at a bank, then a drugstore, then going for his breakfast. He always took the same table near the front window and ordered an omelet. A creature of habit: same order each day, same table, same cheesy lines uttered to waitresses and anyone else too polite to shut down a bore.

Tania had been in the Moonshot Diner twice in the past week. The first time she ignored Price. He had stared at her, and she knew a line was coming. They talked for a bit as she surfed the internet from a laptop; she wasn't all that interested. He didn't take the hint. She left quickly that day and was back the next. By that time, catching Price was easy as reeling in salmon from a spring creek. They spoke at the counter. He asked her out several times. She put him off. Now he was salivating like a stud dog sniffing a poodle's backside.

Today was the day she'd spring the trap.

She'd treated him indifferently today and breakfast was almost over. Price was reading the newspaper, and he rattled the pages as he placed them on the table. He leaned over to her.

"You seem quiet today."

"I had a break-in at my apartment."

This interested him, she could see it. He was the type to monitor the police log for the crime of the day. "Sorry to hear. Back in the day, this neighborhood? No one would dare. Now? Please. No one knows anyone." He trailed off. "They catch the guy?"

"Not yet."

"Too bad. Not a good feeling to have someone in your house like that."

She nodded in agreement. She wondered if Price himself had done a few burglaries over the years. Probably so.

"Any idea who?"

"No."

They sat for a bit while she typed away on an email.

"My old boyfriend was involved in some stuff.

We used to live together. I think it's related to him and his old business."

Price looked at her. "What kind of stuff?"

"I kept out of it. I know he was into some things with the internet and escort sites." She went back to her work.

"Where is he now?"

"Left the state."

"Incarcerated?"

"No, just moved."

"You still see him?"

"No. But I still hear things. From his friends."

"Like what?"

She stared at him but said nothing.

"Sorry to ask, I'm just nosy."

"Some of his business partners are still operating," Tania said. "People are owed money. Other stuff."

Price nodded at this. He ordered another cup of coffee, moving his finger in a little circle over his mug. The waitress hustled over. He acted as if he was ordering a feast at an English countryside castle.

Price looked thoughtful as he swirled sugar into his coffee. "You alright with this?"

"What do you mean?"

"Backlash. Maybe they think you know about the money."

She shook her head. "That's a problem."

"I know a guy you should meet. He might help you with any problems you could have down the road."

"That would be great."

She sat and sipped her coffee while a reality TV show about silicon mob wives with bruised lips burbled in the background.

"What happened with the online business?"

"He got into trouble. Blackmailing people, basically. People who go online, they give over all kinds of information to see the girls. Work address, ID, driver's license."

"Yeah."

"Never knew people were this stupid. He was partners with one or two of these girls who left the business. They used the personal ID info to blackmail the men."

"I see. Smart." Price nodded in admiration.

She nodded and continued. "I still see some girls he used to employ."

"What're they doing now?"

"They're around. Some are working again. I worry about them. That was one thing they had with him. Protection."

Tania could tell Price was pinning back his ears and ready to charge. This was the savannah he knew, working girls to be run down and herded, making him some fair money in the process. He was twitching with excitement, she could sense it.

"This friend in the city could be of help. Let me ask him. He's got good connections."

"You would do that?"

Price smiled. "I like you, Tania. You're a good kid.

And you can use some friends like that." He regarded her with open curiosity. "Don't take it the wrong way, but how did you get to know these people?"

"One of my best friends was a dancer from San Francisco. Performance artist."

He laughed. "That the word now? A stripper?"

She ignored the jibe. "She was more than that. You should have seen her. Jade Apocalypse. She was a trained acrobat and did things in strip clubs that would blow your mind—knives, paint, just unreal body control. I got to know some incredible artistic people through her. She introduced me to my old boyfriend."

Tania knew there was money to be made in men's vices. A recession-proof business, mostly. Men needed their little diversions: sex, drugs, whatever supplied the euphoria of forgetting life for a few hours.

"I don't want this to sound crass, but not everybody operates escort agencies this way."

She just looked at him.

"Some of these places are legit. No shakedown on good customers. And the girls have a safe place to work."

He gave her a card. There was just a name—Venus Baths—and a phone number with a black-and-white drawing of two faceless figures stepping into a tiled bath in the background. She just looked at the card and nodded.

"If those girls are looking around for a better

deal—a safer deal—have them call me." Davin Price, ever the gentleman. "I'll ask my guy to look into what the word is on your boyfriend."

CHAPTER 42

RAY TOOK A back table at The Nite Tripper, a brick and timber joint on Columbus that served up plates of Southern food marinated in authentic blues and jazz. Tania came in a few minutes later and they ordered mojitos heaped with mint leaves and lots of rum.

"So I did some research on that place that Price mentioned, Venus Baths," said Tania. "A reporter I know said there were always rumors that rogue cops were running the place. They knew how escort agencies got busted so they knew how to stay off the radar."

Ray nodded. "Any names?"

"No, not yet."

Ray picked through his fried chicken. The music faded in his mind. "This case reminds me of an old friend," he said. "He was a cop who once worked a beat in Dorchester. Randy Bauman. Quit over a dispute with the brass. He opened a PI agency in the downtown area. One of his first hires was a young investigator who thought he knew everything and learned everything he knew didn't mean shit." He laughed at the thought.

Tania raised her brow. "You?"

"Yes, he was my mentor."

"I thought you were going there."

Ray had loved the guy, and they worked for several years together. Bauman cut against everything expected of cops. He was an instinctive interviewer, able to put people at ease while talking about troubling, embarrassing subjects. He dressed well and didn't give off the shakedown cop vibe. When Ray had first read one of his reports, the witness made so many self-incriminating comments that until he saw the witness testify live, Ray thought Bauman must have fluffed up the remarks. Bauman was among the most subtle, perceptive people he had ever met, seeming to register every body tic or facial expression when he met someone. He knew when to stomp on the gas, when to back off.

Bauman later told Ray why he had been dismissed from the force. Fitzsimmons Shipyard in Southie used to hire a large police security detail, four or five cops each week. It was a cushy job. At some point, the owners cut the security details and installed cameras instead. A group of cops who relied on the extra pay took exception to the decision.

One night, several men cut a fence into the shipyard and trashed the cranes and forklifts used to repair ship hulls. They caused over $50,000 in damage. Bauman went out into the rainy morning to investigate. As he looked around, he noticed a distinctive boot print in the mud: They issued identical boots to the police department. Bauman then saw his career prospects buried. The chief's son had been the moron who trashed the shipyard, and the coverup was on. Everyone knew the department's best detective got sold down the river, part of the patronage cesspool that saw well connected idiots rewarded while talented men got reassigned to Siberia.

Bauman quit the force within a year. To Ray's view, Bauman represented everything he honored in life: a decent man undercut by rats in high places. Ray would never forget what they did to him.

"Get some photos of men coming and going at the massage parlor. If Augustina can ID the cop who's running the place, that would be beautiful." He trailed off. How absurd witness identification was: The entire case could hinge on the accuracy of images embedded in Augustina's brain over fifteen years ago.

"Do you think she's reliable?"

"Reliable as a spiderweb holding back a tank." He shrugged. "But we have more than just her memories."

*   *   *

Over the next few days, Tania continued her investigation. Venus Baths occupied the second floor of an old 1960s office building on Dorchester Avenue.

Chatter on various internet forums suggested the agency charged a premium for clients who wanted uncommon services. She contacted several women who worked in the escort business and told them she wanted to compensate them at their normal hourly rate for a chance to interview them about the business. Two women agreed to meet her. They told Tania disturbing things about the agency. Venus Baths cultivated a niche reputation catering to men who wanted girls to have sex without protection. The clients paid extra for this perk. Girls performed in this manner without complaint. If they complained, then legal issues tended to surface—immigration problems, drug charges, child welfare investigations. The place had strong connections to law enforcement and petty charges acted as a whip over the working girls. Police never raided the agency. There were rumors the agency paid Boston cops off to guarantee the place would never get targeted. One girl who had left the business described a nameless man who seemed to run the place: washed-out face, cold eyes, a serious vibe. He never spoke to anyone but Davin Price, who managed the place day to day. Everyone else gave the man a wide berth. But when this man was around, even Price seemed to act differently, subdued and quieter than he usually was.

Could anyone confirm this man was a Boston cop? No one seemed to know.

Tania sat a block away from Venus Baths on Dot Ave. The silver Honda blended in with every other silver car on the road. Tinted windows, but not too much, just enough to deter a casual glance. Venus Baths occupied a brick building squeezed between a pizzeria and a Vietnamese noodle shop. Price had arrived there in the morning. Around 10 a.m., he stepped out from a rusted side door that opened onto a narrow alleyway, catching Tania by surprise. He hustled through the alley and sat down at a small table set along the wall. She could see there was a second man sitting there already. He wore a tan sport coat over dark pants and thick-soled shoes.

She kept watching and settled into the zen of the street. The normal, crazed traffic on Dorchester Avenue flowed by: Vietnamese women carrying bundled vegetables, an old Irishman in heavy work boots walking from the T station. Cars snaked along amid the toot and holler of an afternoon traffic jam.

After about fifteen minutes, Price and the second man got up from the table and walked through a steel gate to the sidewalk. Price headed across the street, but the other man began walking right toward her, stiff-legged and unsmiling. She could see why no one at Venus Baths talked to him; his pale face was disconcerting, almost inhuman in its stiffness. It was not a face that invited casual conversation. Or any conversation at all.

But she wasn't there for a conversation. She aimed and the camera shutter clicked and clicked and clicked. The man walked past at an angle. He never looked over.

CHAPTER 43

INSIDE HIS APARTMENT, Butters drank beer and thought about what he wanted to say. Then he put in a call to the phone number that McBain had given him.

"Who's this?"

"Joey Butters. Our friend gave—"

"You fucking idiot—"

"I have information that Tommy will want to hear. He can pick me up on Seaport, near the court house. I'll be outside at 4:00 p.m. today."

The voice on the line made noise about this and that, but Butters hung up. He let out a deep breath. It felt good taking the reins. Still, telling Tommy McBain to do something was a strange sensation. He felt a shiver of pleasure run though his spine. Who was in charge now?

He had a few hours to go. Butters walked along the waterfront and mingled with the crowds beneath the arch at Rowes Wharf. Then he walked over the old iron bridge across Northern Avenue and by the courthouse. Everything looked okay. The park was a suitable spot to meet—busy, open. The scale of the blocks was all wrong here, even now after the building boom. There were not enough trees, and the buildings towered over the bare, hard landscape. Even in summer, the wind whipped through the seaport with a Nordic vengeance.

Butters sat down on a bench overlooking the harbor. At some point in your life, you had to make a choice. He was tired of it all, the running, the old neighborhood wars, favors owed, payback demanded. The setup in Revere, the girl in the room, not knowing, it made him sick. He thought of the things he had done that he would never forget. Random acts of casual violence. Witnesses paid off, or worse, humiliating a man with a beat down in front of his children. He prayed for a cleansing fire to rip through his mind and burn away the memories.

It all traced back to that night when Tommy told him to meet by the waterfront. The girl's body in the back seat, her face barely recognizable as a human face. Christ, how had he protected someone who could do that to a girl? And then dumping the whole cauldron over a guy who just chanced to be walking nearby that night. A midnight stroll that altered their lives forever, all three of them.

Once, he had someone in his life who would never have let him become that callous. That was a long time ago.

Butters listened to the steady rhythm as the sea swelled against the jetty. He felt good about what he was doing. He'd talk to McBain like they'd never spoken before, man to man, heart in hand. His life in the crew was over.

He took a cab back to Fleet Street in the North End and got out a few blocks past his place. He could hear the buzz and honk of the restaurant crowds, but all was quiet here.

Butters walked around the block and approached his apartment from the other direction.

He walked into the building and opened up his door. Then arms on either side were lifting him up. He lost his balance. A wet towel jammed his mouth; a hood came down over his head. He yelled as loud as he could, but the noise was just a muffled growl. He felt himself going down to the floor, his head in a dark sea. He struggled to get up and felt something smash into his jaw, then a kick in the stomach. He groaned.

"Stay down," he heard a voice say.

Someone bound his hands behind his back. He heard footsteps and someone clicked on the TV and turned up the volume. They set the channel to an old movie. A dramatic exchange of 1950s voices filled the room.

If he don't show up here, he's in big trouble, mister.

Butters tried to get to his feet. Someone cracked

him hard across the mouth. He felt his lip split and blood ran down his face.

Hey Mack, none of that now.

He sat there and stopped all resistance. For several moments he said nothing, just listened to the burble of the TV show.

He'll done set you straight. You bet he will.

He heard a modern voice from the kitchen. "Christ, you'd think a guy could find a decent American brew in here." It was McBain.

The sound of a refrigerator door closing. Someone ripped the bag off his head, and he felt the edge of it cut his nose. Two hands pulled him to his knees.

He was face-level with two bellies. They belonged to thick men in long shirts that overhung their belts. He noticed the tropical color, a light green, which seemed strange to him. Nothing relaxed about these guys. They clenched his arms.

Then Tommy McBain in his usual black shirt stepped out of the kitchen. He was holding a canvas bag in one hand, a beer in the other. He held the bag away from his tensed body, just slightly, as if there was something inside that he would rather not touch. McBain's dark eyes looked bemused.

"Once again, Joey, you messed it up. You had a chance to do it right." McBain shook his head, and Butters had the odd sense that McBain actually felt disappointed in him. But Butters' attention flew to the canvas bag. It seemed to twist and writhe on its own. Something moved inside.

The TV droned on. *Beam on down to AutoPlanet, and we'll put you in a new Buick today!*

"What happened at the beach, Joey?"

"I don't know."

"What did you tell the PI?"

"Nothing."

Draft and manage football teams from your cell phone! Real time scoring with team highlights.

"What did you tell him about that room in Revere Beach?"

"Nothing. I swear."

"You lie."

"No, I swear. We can work this out—"

McBain backhanded him across the face with a lazy right hand. Then he leaned close.

"You forgot what I said. I do your remembering for you."

"I couldn't, Tommy. She was not supposed to be part of it."

"We do what we need to do. She is involved. You were supposed to nullify her." McBain held the bag up and away from his body. "But you can't even do that right. A little time in the house of corrections is best, Joey."

Butters felt a deep fear surging inside. "No! Oh Jesus—"

Butters was gibbering. McBain gestured and the men held Butters down by his shoulders. He could hardly move for the sheer weight. They forced a wrapped towel back between his jaws.

Then McBain put his beer down. He opened the bag gingerly, pulling back one side and then the other. Butters heard a hissing sound. McBain stepped quickly and shoved the canvas bag over Butters' head like he was trapping a rodent.

Butters went blind. In the darkness, he felt a heavy weight writhe across his shoulders. Something was alive. He felt it whip around his face. All around him a furious hissing. Blind panic set in, something welling up beyond light and understanding. Into the dark cotton wall he screamed, twisting his torso as much as he could. Something ripped into his cheek. His mind lost its moorings in the endless hissing, the swollen blackness. In the distance he could hear a voice screaming and screaming.

CHAPTER 44

RAY WOKE UP early. Outside the window, a soft rain fell. He made some coffee and read the newspaper. The Red Sox were in first place. In the metro section, he stopped the cup of coffee halfway to his lips and swore softly when he saw the name. He scanned the article and then reread it from the beginning.

Man Bitten By Snake Expected to Live

A North End man was bitten numerous times on Thursday night by a pet snake. A concerned neighbor who saw an open apartment door found Joseph Butters, 51, unconscious on the floor of his North End apartment. When the manager and police responded, they found Butters lying on the floor, his face marked by over a dozen bite marks. He was nearly dead when he arrived at MGH, but emergency room personnel were able to treat the wounds and administer antigens to the snake venom that probably saved Mr. Butters' life. "It was touch and go there," said Dr. Peter Fallben. "I've never seen a patient suffer so many bites to the face."

Neighborhood groups are calling for new restrictions in the city on household pets like snakes and reptiles. "These creatures can be deadly to man and that is why they are found in jungles in the first place," said SPP (Sane Pet Policies) Boston Chapter chairperson, Diane Sweetwater. "I hope Mr. Butters recovers. After an incident like this, anyone would agree that reasonable restrictions on such pets are a necessity. Especially in crowded city neighborhoods like the North End."

Authorities confirmed the snake had not been located.

Later that afternoon, Ray finished reviewing old criminal cases involving some men at the bar on the night of the murder. He went for a quick jog and then showered. He pulled on jeans, a white dress shirt, and a pair of boots and took the subway over to the hospital on Charles Street. Thinking back to his first visit with the man, he recalled nothing that showed Butters was the kind of person who owned a snake.

At the hospital, a receptionist told him Butters was on the 8th floor. He took the elevator and stepped out. Floor-to-ceiling windows opened out to a gray sky over the river. He walked inside and saw Butters.

His face and arms were heavily bandaged. He was watching TV and eating a small cup of ice cream. The remains of his dinner lay to the side.

"How you doing?"

"Good."

Ray gestured to the cup. "That a regulation ice cream?"

"Yes. Man, the food is crap here. The venom didn't kill me. But this place will finish the job."

Butters flicked though the TV, stopping at a show about the weekend's preseason football games. The promo started, dramatic music, a robot wearing shoulder pads smashing through a wall as fireworks exploded. Then a camera panned to five thick-necked men packed behind a desk, most of them retired players from a previous generation.

"Five meatheads to break down a game?" muttered Butters.

"They're sharing a brain."

Butters finished his dessert and put the cup down. Ray checked to see if he could open a window, but it was locked. He tried to ignore the hospital stink.

"Snakes are not a common murder weapon. What happened?"

"My pet got loose."

Ray laughed out loud.

"Don't you read the papers, Ray?"

Ray shook his head. "Cops notice you had no food for the snake? No cage?"

Butters clicked the TV again. "I said what I know. My pet got out after throwing a nutter."

"What's your pet's name, Magnus?"

Butters' upper body grew rigid.

"And the guy with dick problems—McBain. You know him, too?"

Butters looked at Ray. "Why do you say that?"

"Any guy who beats up women seems to have problems with his dick. It all stems from that. That's why they take out their anger on women."

"You a psychiatrist?"

"I'm a truth teller. I read his prior cases. There is a theme running through his past."

Butters looked up at the TV screen. "I feel bad for your guy. I do. But this is what I gotta live with."

Ray felt disgust well up in his belly. He thought of his father, his involvement in the old Mafia trials. How many other men were in the same position? Decent men with families who lived simple lives, cafe owners, small business people who grew up in certain neighborhoods and never escaped the dark orbit of the gangs. Men whose lives were swinging on a chain held by someone like Butters. There was a rumor of a fish-monger who had gone missing at the time; the poor guy had delivered seafood to a mansion on the day the feds conducted a massive raid. Because he was at the mansion, he was arrested and later released. Some goon concluded he must have tipped off the feds, and the man disappeared a year later, never to be seen again. That was how business was handled in that era.

Ray was never sure where to direct his rage: his father, the gangsters, or the police. For a long time he had decided it should be his father. The father who was not there, the father who quit being one when he ended his life. But years later, he had found forgiveness in the stories repeated by those who knew his father, who knew the real man behind the image. A man who was loved by his neighbors, who remembered his friendly banter as a blessed thing, the warmth of his smile and the little gifts he gave to friends and strangers alike. Ray wasn't so sure anymore. Anger was a rich cocktail, and the passing of time wears away all things.

Ray knew he was at the end of the road with Butters. He moved to the bedside and turned to Butters, who was fixing him with a curious look.

"I can't say I've seen someone unleash a snake before. I can only tell you my guy has been inside for fifteen years. That's worse than a hundred snakes ripping into you. And you think they will just forget you? I can't make you tell me anything. But we need you."

"You think the snake meant to leave me alive?" Butters said.

Ray sat back and shook his head. "Keep moving forward, Joey. It's the only way you find out the cost of what you're running from."

Butters' eyes held a sad, glazed look. He clicked through the television channels and didn't say a word. Ray sat and watched him, trying to decipher his mood. Then he stood up. He felt the anger building, but he didn't want to say anything that would mar the tenuous relationship. He reached out a hand. Butters took it in a hard grip.

"I'm sorry. I know what you need. But can't do it," Butters said.

"What hurts you today will hurt you again tomorrow," Ray said.

Butters cast his gaze down to his lap. Ray left the room.

CHAPTER 45

FEELING HIS ANGER building to a blowout, Ray left the hospital and walked up Cambridge Street toward City Hall, stomping the pavement to work off his frustration. He stopped at a bar with windows flung open to the late summer. He ordered a glass of Sicilian wine, a Nero D'Avola, and hunkered over a back table to mull over options. Augustina was still in. But he needed more evidence, more witnesses. Butters seemed resigned to dying with his secret. He was a man destined for a lifetime of lonely walks on a rotten pier. Butters could not bring himself to care enough to act, even when the need was clear. Wallowing in his weakness.

Ray knew these cases could make one almost physically ill at times. The road to redemption was always just out of reach, human weakness littered everywhere, splayed out for all to see.

He sipped the wine and looked up at the TV. In a preseason game, the Detroit Lions were moving the football, a rarity in this decade. But the defense converged on a fourth down play, burying the running back in a silver and blue Patriot sea. The crowd went bonkers, and the planets moved back to their customary alignment.

He finished his drink and made the decision. He dialed Tania.

"We are going to interview Price tonight. Can you get those photos together in an hour?"

"Sure."

"You have his cell, right? Call him and get him out of his cave. Let's get him to the Park Plaza, tell him you'll meet at the bar in the lobby. Time for the show. Let me know as soon as you hear."

They discussed the plan. Tania would make the call but keep it brief. Men reacted to cryptic messages from a woman. They misread all the signs and assumed they were going to end up in bed. Ray suspected Price would snap the bait.

He sat for another twenty minutes and watched the game. Then Tania rang his cell again.

"He's happy to meet me on short notice," she said.

"Of course he is." They discussed their approach one more time and agreed to meet in an hour.

Ray packed his briefcase and then tapped his phone for a ride. A Honda sedan pulled up and took him to the hotel. Ray got out and took a seat near an entrance.

Tania had arrived early. He could see her now at a quiet table in the lobby bar. She looked incredible, aristocratic, with her hair pulled back in a pony-tail. She was dressed in a black skirt, low strappy heels, and a light blue blouse. Tania meant business. Price just didn't know what kind. A piano player finger-danced on the keys and a low melody filled the old marble lobby. Large potted ferns surrounded each table and extended patrons a semblance of privacy. A perfect scene.

Price strode in from the front entrance, dressed in a tattered black shirt with a Hawaiian motif, blue jeans, and boat shoes. He was aiming to cut the look of a yacht owner, but sullen seams around his eyes hinted at darker trade than mere pleasure cruises. He spotted Tania at the table and perked up. All of Price's defenses were down. He walked quickly toward her, pulling his shirt tighter across his chest. Ray laughed to himself. Some things never changed. Men got roped like fattened cattle when a woman paid a little attention.

He watched as Tania lit Price up with a warm smile and soon the pair were engaged in soft banter over the table. Price made some grand, sweeping gestures with his hands, a man of the world at ease in marble lobbies at grand hotels. A waiter came and then brought over their order: white wine for her, a whiskey for him. He was leaning over the table, his arm dangling like a crab claw. He was going for it, marking time until he could brush against Tania's arm. She saw her opportunity. Tania said something in a low voice and Price began staring at a folder on the table with a look of puzzlement crossing his face. Tania said something else. Price froze. Then she opened the folder. She began showing him the photographs, one after another. Price's eyes grew wide. He looked around the lobby as if nerves were jutting out like hot wires from his forehead.

Ray got up and moved to the table.

"Hi Davin," Ray said. "Please sit, we just want to talk."

Price glared at Tania and Ray. "You better talk," he muttered. He hunched over the edge of his chair. "What the fuck is this?" He pointed to the photos. "Someone following me around?" His voice was tense and his neck swiveled, looking for the cavalry charge.

Ray looked at him and gestured to the table. "Please, let's just sit down and talk for a minute."

Price settled down once he saw it was just Ray and Tania at the table. "So this is all a setup?" Price stared at Tania.

She fixed him with a steady gaze. "No cops. This is what I had to do to get you out here to talk."

"Fucking A." Price shook his head in disgust.

"You remember me?" Ray asked.

"I do," Price said, licking his lips.

Ray picked up one photo and got right to the point. "I know you couldn't talk the first time. But I told you what was going down. The investigation into Sam Langford's case is near the end. I don't know what you remember about the case, but we have enough to file. I know about Butters. He covered for McBain. And we have other witnesses. I know Magnus forced a witness, a woman, to lie on the stand. But what you may not know is that two cops assaulted her, raped her."

"So what? I don't talk to cops. I got my reputation in this town—"

"It's all coming out now." Ray continued on like he never heard a word. "Once we appeal and this evidence comes out in a criminal case, it will be a nightmare for the police department. They don't want to take many more hits. Once we show that rapists are on the city payroll, the DA will indict."

Ray paused and lowered his voice.

"You are not important here. Your role was limited. We started looking into the Venus club because we heard it was run by dirty cops. That is the big story. Now we know that the cop running the club—I'm talking about Magnus, just to be clear—is the same cop who raped female witnesses over fifteen years ago. I think you can see what's going to happen."

Ray stopped as a waitress serviced the table and asked for drink orders. Ray smiled at her and ordered a glass of Chianti. Tania ordered another drink. Price hesitated but then ordered a second whiskey. He sat back. His eyes kept drifting to the photographs.

Ray took out his phone, pulled up a news article, and put it in front of Price. "They feel the pressure, Magnus and McBain. Take a look at this." He pointed to the story of Butters being rushed to the hospital after being bitten in the face by a snake. "Take a minute and read. This is what they did to Butters. Interesting. You'd think we lived in Miami. Snakes are a real problem."

He paused while Price read the article with his chin in his hand, elbow on the table. He sighed and scratched his cheek. Ray noticed how lined Price's face was, like a leather mask that he pulled on each morning. He looked tired. For the first time, Ray could sense that Price was wavering.

"So why is this all coming back now?"

"Langford is appealing his case and witnesses will testify. So Magnus is pruning off weak branches. They tried to get to her. And then tried to get Butters. Maybe you're next."

Price looked out across the bar to another table where a young family was looking over a menu. He grew quiet. For the next hour, Ray and Tania let Price absorb the information, drink his whiskey, ask questions. He grew angry and resigned, and at one point, Ray could see some patrons looking over at the table with a curious stare. Still, Ray and Tania pressed him.

"You ever think, Davin, just how you parachute out of this thing? How does it end for you? Magnus will live off a city pension, plus the cut he gets from your guys. The top guys like McBain run the rackets. What do you actually make a year doing this shit?"

Price shrugged. He looked ashen. "I've been thinking there might come a time like this."

"Like what?" asked Tania.

"If McBain or Magnus got that amped up to take out Butters, anyone could be next."

"So get out in front of this," said Ray. "The DA will deal with the first one who comes over the bridge. Lay it out. It should be you. Time to cut loose."

Ray and Tania worked over the evidence with Price again, about how Sam Langford had done over a decade of time for a crime he did not commit. Price took a deep breath.

"Look, I don't care about your appeal, to be honest. But this was always dirty business at the bar. He was gonna go down for this."

"Who?"

"Tommy McBain. That thing that happened at the Electric House was not sanctioned business, obviously. That was McBain going on a fuckin' bender. He used up a lotta juice to get himself out. And Magnus was working for us back then. But that's not true anymore."

"How do you mean?"

Price shrugged. "Magnus calls his own shots now."

Ray and Tania said nothing. Price sat back and sipped his whiskey.

"McBain can go fuck himself on this," he said finally. He exhaled. "Help get me numbers from the DA, and I'll see what I can do."

"Why me? I'm not a lawyer. I can't represent you."

"Yeah, but you're the one making things happen right now. I don't deal direct with cops or DAs." Price rubbed his lips.

Ray thought for a moment. "I will intervene. But there's something you can do to smooth the way."

CHAPTER 46

McBAIN STOOD AT the head of the table in the back office at the Electric House, beer in hand, rock music playing just loud enough to be heard without him yelling. He was back from checking the office of Castlehaven Investments, located inside the basement of a decrepit apartment building just off Broadway. The crew was running a classic boiler room scam after McBain got a prospect list from a disbarred broker—the list was all high rollers the guy had porked when working at a legitimate New York investment firm. His crew targeted new-issue whores, buyers who could not resist the lure of a cold call with a hot tip. The penny stocks they were selling were worthless—until Castlehaven Investments pumped them up. McBain recruited some smooth-throated lads from the neighborhood and taught them the phone routine. He even had two Brits on the phones. Americans loved buying from brokers with British accents. Castlehaven had fake websites and shiny brochures on excellent quality stock. They called the targets from an 800 number that was linked to a large New York brokerage firm, explaining to the targets that all trades from Castlehaven were cleared by the bank. So far, they had eased off over $800,000 from a dozen buyers. Once the price hit a high point, they'd dump the stock and close down the whole thing within the week, strip the place of any trace they were ever there. He had already transferred the funds around to various accounts in Cyprus and the Isle of Man.

Not for the first time, McBain admired the power of the internet. Thanks to computers, ripping off rich people had become a decidedly less violent activity in the last decade. This showed, to his mind, the potential of humanity to evolve as new rackets emerged. Hacked email accounts, meth, Molly, passwords— there was always a connect, someone who mainlined into the vein of the next big thing, shot it full of poison, and watched it collapse. And then something new came along.

But it was time to turn back to an old problem. They still did not know how to stop the Langford investigation. They had botched the hit on Infantino in the Chelsea warehouse district. The PI was still nosing around, building a case for Langford, kicking up old bones. And even though Butters was decommissioned after the chat in his apartment, the girl Augustina was still lurking out there.

McBain was furious. He could see that the other

men around the table were picking up on his mood. Maybe a few felt fear. He saw Davin Price was sucking cigarettes like they were oxygen straws.

"So what's the play?" he asked. "I come from watching money flow to talking about the one thing you fucks can't fix."

"We're going to let things sit with the girl," Price said. "We know where she is and where she's going. She will not be a problem."

Ted Spurr leaned his axe-shaped face into view. "I'd like to add something here." Spurr was always a fucking diplomat. He had set up the investment scam and was always good for an idea or three, running the gamut of the crazy, the bad, and the brilliant. "You want to be certain on this, Tommy. I mean, we know everything there is to know. She could go away any time. Space up there on the North Shore. Remember that thing in Salem, the Benfanto crew? There's burial space there still, we know the guy. Night job. Shovel her in, backfill, done." Spurr snapped his fingers. "No one the wiser."

McBain frowned at him. "I don't think so. Too many eyes right now. That goes too far."

He shook his head. There had been a time when these things were taken care of expediently. No rush, just an eventuality about it. He gave the crew what they needed to know, they made their bones when they found an opportunity. Now, it was a different scene. Rats were running loose everywhere in the family home and you trusted no one. Those close to you, even less. They contracted the street work to Mexican and Black gangs. The whole thing was so far from the majesty of what it once was. Or what the old timers told him it once was. Now, the rackets were a goddamn mess, riddled with informers and led by dickless wonders.

"What's the Iceman say on this?" asked Spurr.

McBain frowned. "He arrested her years ago. Gave her a hard talking to. Surprised she's still around flapping her goddamn cakehole. So keep looking at options."

Price slogged back a beer and went out to the bar. He glanced down at his shirt. He was sweating and picked at his shirt as he walked back to the office. Price lit another cigarette.

Spurr was just explaining how shooting someone with a .22 under the jawline was better than using a .357 because the slug, instead of exiting, rattled around the skull and scrambled the brain. Some men sat back at this, genuinely impressed.

* * *

A few blocks away, Ray sat in an office inside an unobtrusive brick building in the South End with a detective from the Boston Police Department. Located a few blocks from headquarters, the building housed a few special units such as internal affairs and special investigations. The office was open and airy, which surprised him. It seemed more like the office of an architect or a graphic designer, not a warehouse containing a mountain of boxes with evidence of serious crimes committed by police officers.

Price and Ray had negotiated the details of his cooperation agreement, and it had not been a simple process. Price refused to wear a wire. But he agreed to something else. A few weeks after the meeting at the hotel, a judge signed off on a wiretap of the Electric House. One evening, Price and Tania stopped in at the Electric House for a few drinks. It was a Monday night, and the bar was quiet. Most of the crew were recovering from a weekend of plunder and excess. The back office, off-limits to anyone but McBain and the crew, was locked, as usual. Price got up to use the men's room. When he got back, he pointed Tania to the restroom near the office, which he had just left unlocked. She only needed five minutes. While Price had sipped a beer and looked around, Tania slipped inside the office. She took out a screwdriver and detached a wall outlet, then re-attached one outfitted with a microphone. The police had dozens of hours of audio now. They were hearing many references to someone called the Iceman.

Ray convinced one of the detectives to let him listen in on the wiretap so he could add to the profile police were developing. The slow process was grating on his nerves but he tried to remain patient.

"The Iceman," said the detective. "There's another reference to him."

"That's Magnus, I'm telling you. He runs this guy McBain," Ray said. "Has for years."

They listened to more discussion. Nothing significant. Ray sipped a coffee and jotted down some notes while the detective tinkered with the volume.

"When they go in, will they smack Price around a bit to make it look legit?" Ray asked.

The detective laughed. "We do that anyway."

* * *

Ray sat in a steel chair and sipped the last dregs of a dark coffee. It was getting late. There had been no major revelations today.

Word was the raid might come tonight or tomorrow. The entire crew was there. No stragglers. The crew had gone off into discussing ongoing business, some of it so mundane Ray and the cop had to laugh out loud. What kind of meat was going to be served at the Labor Day party? Should they expand the selection of Irish beers?

Then McBain brought up a federal case where a crew member was running into a problem with his partner, a restaurateur who was under subpoena in a federal trial. The restaurateur was the public face of the business and there was a fear he was going to turn into a songbird.

McBain said, "Take care of it. Handle it like we did on that other thing, the cafe."

There was silence from the room.

"A few years ago, there was a cafe owner on Hanover Street who was starting to become a problem."

Ray felt a chill run through him. 89 Hanover Street was his father's old place. He had checked into the chain of title years ago, curious about what names might surface; all the names seemed to be legitimate owners. Was McBain or Magnus behind the frame-up all those years ago? What were the odds that this crew was running a cafe in the same spot? His mind raced with possibilities.

"Old man killed himself. How long has it been, fifteen, twenty years?"

"Yeah, I remember that."

"We will feed the feds what they want to hear."

Another voice chimed in. "Just dilute the whole fucking thing. Get some names of some people and sprinkle them around. Muck it up. Set it up so the guy is unusable as a witness."

"Have the Iceman come up with a way to video these card games where the old timers bet," McBain said. "Make sure the restaurant guy is there, too. We'll confuse the jury. And if the owner kills himself like the old Italian, even better."

There was a roll of laughter around the group. Ray's chest felt as if a vice were tightening on his ribcage. Magnus was going to place the owner into the mix, just like he had done years ago to his father. It had to be his father they were discussing, he was certain. All these years later, they still were running the same scam. He felt lightheaded, as if he were walking in a dream. He struggled to keep his breathing steady and deep.

For another hour, Ray listened as the hidden microphone sent the words of the gangsters into the audio recorder. The detective made occasional comments and Ray replied as if he were listening. His mind was a million miles away now. He got up to leave and stayed calm. "I'm heading out. That seems it for tonight."

The cop looked over at him. "Some good stuff. We will see where it goes."

Ray nodded, went outside, and walked a block away to make sure no one would overhear him.

Ray called Tania. "What address did you get on Magnus?"

"He lives in Dorchester." She told him the address, and he tapped it into his phone. He felt pure rage flowing through his body. His skull felt compressed, as if it were heated with hot gas. "Is everything okay?"

"Just overheard something. Magnus was connected to my father's case. Right from the mouth of McBain."

"What? Ray, you can't go over there! They're right in the middle of the investigation."

He knew she was right but he couldn't control himself. "He set up my father. This gets handled now." Ray's hands were shaking. He had one chance to get in some retaliation.

CHAPTER 47

RAY JOGGED TO his Jeep, fired up the engine, and started driving. He thought back to his teenage years. All those years, how wrong he had been about his father. For the longest time, he directed his anger one way, lancing only his father. His father had given in. Given up. Quit on his own family. For so many years, there was no one else Ray could blame.

But now there was another name searing his brain: Scott Magnus. The fraudulent man in blue. Ray would make Magnus ride the lightning for what he did.

His mother had died when he was just five, so he had only shards of images of her in his mind. As a child, he knew his father in that simple way that all children know their parents—the father who worked all day and arrived home, arms laden with food. A man who shook off the cold on Christmas Eve and took his son out to walk the streets of the North End, pushing small gifts and candies into the hands of neighbors and anyone else he found in the street. These were the broad strokes devoid of shading by which he knew his father.

As he grew into adulthood, he saw for the first time how life could treat a gentle person.

His father, Leo, ran a cafe in the North End, a simple place, espressos and cappuccinos, a lunch counter with panini and pasta dishes. There was a cozy, wood-paneled room in back for private parties and special customers. It was well known that some of the neighborhood Mafioso ate at the cafe and fraternized in the back room. Ray's uncle had warned his father to keep his distance from these men, but Leo wouldn't turn anyone away. "These guys, they have to eat, too," his father said. "What do I do, tell a good customer no?"

When federal agents indicted several mafiosi based on tips from an informant, they shotgunned the indictment to implicate his father despite not a shred of evidence tying him to organized crime—except his last name had the right number of vowels. The feds leaned on him. They pressed him in the way a massive organization can bring sheer power on a smaller opponent to force an outcome. They wanted him to testify about conversations in the back room, while Mafia bosses warned him to forget everything about the back room. The police made a claim that they had tapes of the bosses at the games, with betting slips showing his father taking a cut of the action.

A rumor spread that he was going to be named a defendant in a revised complaint.

Together, the Mafia and the feds ground down his father, pounding and pounding him like a piece of metal, shaping him into a depressed, fearful old man, thinned and flattened into a thing without resistance, no longer resembling the original element. His father announced he was closing the cafe. And then, on the last day after clearing the last table and sweeping up, he went to the basement and shot himself in the head.

At the church, Ray stood in the pew like a zombie, his chest throbbing, listening to words from his father's friends and customers, missives of grief and love passing by his head like crows in a windstorm. Sorry for your loss. Sorry for what they did to him... Sorry sorry sorry. The old man was gone, and he was alone now.

The funeral ended, and he walked behind the casket out the church doors. He rested his right hand on the wood. It was his last walk with his father. Then he heard his uncle step toward him and say something. Something in his uncle's voice was breaking, and it frightened him. There was a hollow edge to it he had never heard before.

"Ray, he was the best man in this neighborhood. He didn't always agree with the little guy. He just hated the big guy. And now it comes to this. They killed him."

Ray knew his father and uncle had no resources in a battle between whales. His rage built and built until he got home later that day and then everything he felt overflowed his bulwarks. He broke down in tears, away from everyone, sobbing uncontrollably in his apartment. The police and the gangsters fought on and on, making money, making careers, while they trampled ordinary people in their wake.

He drove the Jeep hard over to lower Blue Hill Avenue, past the iron-barred windows of housing developments, past a moonlit field dedicated to another teenage shooting victim, past crumbling storefront churches in Grove Hall and out past the rambling stone walls lining Franklin Park. By the time he got to Dorchester's Lower Mills district, prowling the street for parking, he was jumping out of his skin. All his senses pointed to the target.

Ray pulled off onto a side street and flicked off the indicator lights inside the car. He took a deep breath and let it out. He needed to maintain some sense of control. Ray reached behind him for a leaded sap he kept in the back of the car for certain times of need and slid it into his pocket.

He walked past a parking lot to a brick warehouse that a developer had converted to condominiums. Magnus lived here. It was late, and beneath a stand of pine trees shadowing the parking lot, Ray saw several benches arranged around a fountain. He sat down on one that commandeered a view of the building and took out his phone, pretending to be busy with messages.

Beneath the trees, the air was dark and pine

scented. Fifteen minutes passed by. Nothing happened. In a distant part of his mind, Ray realized this was a stupid thing he was doing. But in the end, the tracker chose his illusion, followed it to the end. He chose blood and family and justice, and would go on until it all broke apart in the end.

A thrill rushed along the base of his skull. He watched a middle-aged man with pale skin and cold, flat eyes open the heavy wooden door and move across the parking lot. He recognized him. Magnus was looking at his phone, not paying attention.

Ray shook his head. Even an old cop acted like a dope nowadays, walking in darkness while playing with his cell phone. The lack of finesse appalled him.

Why not now?

Ray slid off the bench. The night receded before his eyes and a ghost light seemed to outline his target as if on a stage. He was completely focused on the shape of Magnus in front of him. The small muscles moved in Magnus' forearm as he texted someone on his phone. He paused as he reached for his car.

Ray moved. This was for the old cafe owner, his father Leo, for everything that got taken away. He glided behind and then cracked the sap across the side of Magnus' skull, just below the ear. Magnus went down, moaning in pain and raising his elbows to protect his face.

Ray heard or saw the phone skitter across the pavement. Magnus moaning in pain, the man who had all but pulled the trigger and killed his father.

He felt a bone-deep jolt upon seeing this piece of shit down on the ground. It was maddening. He didn't want it to end. The guttural need was too much. He would take something out of Magnus tonight.

He bent to his task, whipping the sap hard across the face and neck, quick, snapping blows over and over until the once-pale face looked like bruised tomatoes. Magnus wasn't even fighting back now; he seemed barely conscious. Ray continued to pound away on Magnus, a cold dance that had no end. Then he switched the sap to his left hand and punched Magnus in the face.

Then Ray saw Tania running at him from the street. She was reaching her arms out, and he felt it as a fever dream, this dark angel reaching out to him as he was about to do some horrible thing to another person, something that might stain him forever.

His face turned to the sky, and the darkness rolled back from his eyes. The world around him dropped its muffler, and he heard her voice and some other sound, a wailing. He smelled the smell of asphalt and knew he had lost it. His breath came in ragged gasps.

He looked around like a man waking from a long sleep. An iron gate surrounded the parking lot. The dark trunks of maples lined the red brick of the warehouse. Tania was there, and they were alone with his crime.

"You have to get out of here."

Ray looked at the red-smeared sap in his hand.

Tania grabbed his arm. "Just leave him. People are coming. Where's your car?"

"Off the avenue."

"Let's take mine, it's closer."

He tucked the sap into his pocket and shuffled after her. Tania led the way down a path away from the gate, along the street and into a tree-lined yard. She took a brick path that ran behind the warehouse. They passed beneath a light pole on the path and ascended a stone stairway that opened up on a bridge behind the warehouse. He heard the rushing water of a brook and imagined washing the blood off his hands.

Tania and Ray walked to her car and got in. She drove away and headed toward Milton. The three-decker apartments that lined the streets thinned out as they drove into the leafy suburbs. Large Colonial homes with wide sidewalks passed by. Gigantic oaks and maples shaded the roadway. Landscaped lawns and stone walls replaced the fences of the less pricy neighborhoods. Ray could feel the blood slowing in his veins.

Tania drove in silence for a while and Ray was glad for it. He felt not embarrassed, but something else, like a hidden, cancerous part of him was now jutting out in the open, a part that neither one of them was sure how to handle.

"Should we call an ambulance? Make an anonymous call? He's hurt."

He didn't answer her. Tania sighed and dialed 911 from a spoof phone number. She gave an address and said that someone was down in the parking lot. She hung up before the questions started.

Tania looked over at Ray with concern in her eyes. "I've never seen you like that. It was frightening. I thought you were going to kill him."

"That was the goal." He laughed. He told her more about what he had heard about Magnus' role in his father's case. "When I heard that address come across the receiver, it was too much. I never knew that. I just lost it."

He looked out the window. Neatly tended homes, traditional Colonials or Tudors, slid by on the wealthy streets of Milton.

"I left that place on short notice and I think the cop is going to put it together. This could be bad."

Tania kept driving. "Unless they don't know the significance of the address."

Ray thought about it. Would the detective piece together that the cafe owner was his father? An allusion to it was right there on the tape. But the police didn't necessarily know the history.

Tania kept driving and seemed to work up to something. "You need some help, Ray."

He looked at the blood dripping down his pant leg. It was hard to argue with her.

"What goes through your head when something like that happens?"

"It's more what doesn't go through. Thoughts. Calmness. It's pitch black, underwater. Everything goes silent and I just react."

"Your anger is out of control. How can you do that to someone? You fight against people who use violence. Yet in the end, you use the same methods they do."

"It's for a noble cause," he said. "You see how that works. The mind can justify anything."

He intended it as a joke, but Tania wasn't laughing.

CHAPTER 48

PRICE STOOD UP again, a cigarette dangling from his lips. He walked outside to the bar and turned down the stereo. Then he came back to the office and sat down. There was a pause in the conversation, and he looked up. McBain was staring at him. "Why did you do that?" he asked.

Price looked at McBain. "What?"

"Turning down 'Astral Weeks' will get you killed around here."

A couple of guys laughed. Price got back up and headed back to the bar. Spurr yelled down the hallway, "Davin, you big pussy. You wear ear plugs at the concerts now? Just prance out there and put on some Beyonce."

Price turned up the volume and sat back down at the table. "Gotta preserve the jelly. You had any left between those ears, you'd be looking after it, too."

McBain liked that. Spurr needed to get his ass busted once in a while.

McBain turned, and they went back to work. There was a new law being debated on Beacon Hill that would legalize marijuana. It seemed almost guaranteed to become law at some point, and McBain and the others knew it would gut profits in that sector. How were they going to manage this? Spurr said that protection money was down because dealers were leaving the market. And those dealers would never return to the business now that anyone could go to a marijuana dispensary and purchase cannabis in any of a dozen legal, dope-laced products. Getting high was becoming so easy, it was depressing. But Spurr had some ideas.

"I think we need to invest in more flake. That shit is never going to be legalized. It's a foolproof industry. It kills people. So there's a stigma there. You're always gonna have street dealers for that kind of product."

Someone suggested finding new ways to expand the OxyContin trade, which was a great drug: addictive and expensive. Spurr thought there was a way to not just steal the product but to use a couple of dirty doctors up in Lawrence to write hundreds of phony prescriptions for ghost patients in return for a cut. McBain liked the idea and told them to look into expanding this line of business.

Outside, sirens sliced into the night air. McBain got up to look outside with a bored look on his mug. He walked out to the bar. Several of the men followed him to a window. Blue lights rotated across the windows. Five squad cars pulled hard into the lot, a roiling blue mass blocking the entrance. He saw cops rolling out in numbers.

McBain frowned. This was never supposed to happen. They knew people. Maybe the early warning system was getting slack. They paid certain people well to get advance notice on this kind of shit. Someone was going to pay for the screwup.

Now cops were moving toward the bar with weapons drawn. This was something new. This was not good. Inside the bar, a panicky buzz permeated the air. One or two of the men with restraining orders and outstanding warrants tried to make it out the back door. He heard a door slam and glass breaking somewhere. He looked outside as burly cops tackled two of his men to the ground.

McBain's instincts were to sit still and let the cops think he had it all under control. Which he did. Then he thought of his cell phone. He reached inside his jacket and started deleting the call logs.

The cops were heading to the back room already.

"GET YOUR FUCKIN' HANDS UP!"

McBain tapped away and deleted a few calls. Shouting nearby, loud over the music, Van Morrison still doing his thing. There was yelling and glass breaking and he saw Spurr overturn a table and try to make a barricade. But his belly wrap of fat slowed him and some young ninja cop hurtled over the table and crashed into him. Spurr began clubbing the side of the man's face with his fist and both men fell, twisting down to the floor.

McBain moved toward the bar. A young cop yelled at him to stop and put his hands up, but McBain ignored the command. When the cops came around the bar, McBain resisted a little for old times' sake. He didn't want them to think he was retired, or not paying attention. One of them deserved a crack in the head. He delivered a haymaker on the first cop, a giant who he had seen walking on Broadway when he was younger. This kid was built like a maple tree, and he just barreled into McBain and knocked him down. McBain struggled with the giant, but it was useless. He was cuffed in seconds.

McBain felt someone else walk toward him and hold him down. He twisted his neck a bit and tried to look up. There was a short, muscular guy with dark skin on top of him. He looked at the face. It was a Chinese cop, of all things. He knew it was going to be different this time.

His face was flat on the beer-stained wood floor and he could see Price across the room, being braced in a chair by two cops. The blue horde soon had the place under control.

McBain noticed something. While Price was in cuffs, he was the only member of the crew not restrained by one of those oversized, steroid-abusing cops. His mind ran to the conversation earlier and how Price had sauntered over to kill the volume on the stereo. With a sickening snap, the lock fell into place.

"You fuckin' rat," he snarled. Price looked away.

The Chinese cop looked down. "Careful now, Tommy."

McBain knew that if Price had flipped, the dance was over.

The Chinese cop, or whatever he was, interrogated him. McBain spat on the floor and some spittle glistened on the man's black leather boots.

"That will cost you, motherfucker," said the cop. Then he smiled.

McBain wanted to goad the guy into overreacting, get into a bit of a dustup. But this cop was steady, too calm to be baited. McBain tried to build up some rage at the dark face, but it wasn't the same as when the cops were all Irish. He wanted to fight someone who looked like him, someone who understood that the street where they grew up had two sides, and choices had to be made. McBain just shook his head. It was a different era, and Father Time couldn't be beat.

He let out a sigh. "I want my lawyer."

CHAPTER 49

THE MORNING AFTER the raid, Ray got up, made coffee, and took a cup out with him to the patio. He thought back to what had happened with Magnus. Tania had dropped him off at his car later and he had driven home. He slept a few hours. Had he ruined everything with that impulsive decision to deal with Magnus? For now, all was quiet. In his own mind, he still felt no guilt over the beating. But the impulsiveness of the decision bothered him.

He showered, put on a blue pinstripe suit and black wingtips, and headed to the prison in Walpole. The guards shunted him through the steel and cement holding pens, a piece of legal cargo moving to an ultimate destination. If they were aware of what happened yesterday, they gave no sign. This time, Ray declined one of the cramped attorney rooms and set up at an empty table near a sunny window. Then he waited.

A few minutes later, he heard a steel door slide

open and the clinking of chains. Langford walked across the floor with a wary look in his eye. They shook hands and sat down in the hard plastic chairs.

"We meeting out here?" asked Langford.

"Yes, I thought it might be fine for today," said Ray, gesturing to the window. "The sun seemed a better option."

Langford nodded.

"Listen, I don't want to promise too much here, but I have some news. You may be on the road out of here."

Sam stood up as if he thought someone had boo-by-trapped the table. "You serious?" The guard gazed over and Ray shook his head, everything was fine.

"Police raided the Electric House last night. They cleaned house."

"Good Lord. If that's true, maybe they have something." Langford sat back down and let out a breath of air.

"They arrested McBain and five other men. They're going to be arraigned for the murder of Katie Donnegan. Conspiracy, extortion, drugs, weapons possession, you name it. And there is more going on that will take a while to sort out. The feds are investigating the role of Magnus and certain Boston Police officers."

"So what's next?"

"Stone is in court right now trying to get a judge to order your release. Butters never found it in him to help. But Augustina is on board. She will testify that police raped her and forced her to testify falsely. They set you up that night. McBain saw you walking alone. Then Magnus forced her to lie and put you at the scene."

Sam shook his head. He was dazed. "This is really happening."

"Yes. The DA will have to be sold on Augustina. They'll interview her again, check her story out. But she's solid."

"She is with us?"

"Yes. Once they see everything she says checks out, Stone will push for a judge to order your release."

"And Magnus?"

"That's going to be a long battle. Augustina identified him after one of my investigators got photos of him. She also identified him in an old photo we got from Butters' ex-girlfriend. Magnus will deny and deny. But both the city and the feds will see the evidence that shows how far up his ass the Irish mob had crawled. That boy is rotten. BPD is going to want to act fast, keep it in-house, before the feds come in and embarrass them."

He did not mention what had happened to Magnus.

Sam sagged as if a gargantuan weight was rolling off him. "I won't be able to stand it." He fell into his arms on the desk.

"What?"

"If it doesn't happen. So many false starts over the years. Motions for trials, hearings, all that shit.

This time, this time, it has to happen. It's like some-one dangles a piece of meat in front of the bars and you lunge for it—"

Ray stood up and put his arm around Sam's shoulders. He noticed the guard stir, looking in, ready to act on behalf of the state to tamp down any gesture of human warmth. The guard muttered something about no contact.

Ray stepped back. The ways to degrade were endless.

Sam's hands were shaking as he stood there. "Everything you're doing, I can't thank you enough."

Ray shook his hand. "We're not there yet. Justice never sleeps. But it dozes off for long periods of time."

He stood, walked to the door, and spoke to the guard.

"Sorry I reached over to him. He just got some good news today. He's okay now." The guard, a young guy, didn't seem too interested in busting his ass about the rules violation. He waved it off. Langford just nodded, trying to take it all in. Then the guard led Langford out of the room and walked him back down the hallway.

* * *

Ray, Tania, and the defense team filed into court for the hearing on whether Sam Langford would walk out of jail. The Assistant District Attorney for Suffolk County was Timothy Gleason, a solid prose-cutor who checked off all the boxes: baseball coach, yellow Lab, receding hair, late-model American car, a not-too-young, devoted wife. He got up to address the judge. To no one's surprise at the defense table, the government would make their usual arguments, more interested in the finality, as opposed to the accuracy, of the original incorrect decision. But Gleason seemed to only go at it half way. This was Gleason's reward for being a junior man in the office: making arguments to keep an innocent man in prison for just a little while longer.

Stone laid out the complete story, the backdrop to Augustina's coerced confession: Cahill's harassment campaign, her arrest at the supermarket, Magnus raping her in the backseat of a prowl car. How Price and Butters offered Langford as a sacrificial lamb, placing him at the murder of Katie Donnegan and drawing attention away from McBain.

"Perhaps the state has forgotten that the presumption of innocence is still a standing principal under the Constitution," Stone pointed out. "The evidence will show Sam Langford was wrongfully convicted. He is innocent. There is no flight risk here, Your Honor. Once the court has heard all the evidence, and weighed the merits of that evidence, we will request that this court order the release of Mr. Langford immediately.

"Your Honor, I would like to call my first witness."

Then he looked back at Ray and nodded. Ray got up and hastened through the doors into the hallway. He walked over to a bench and sat down next to Augustina. Dressed up in a dark blue dress with a white blouse, she sat alone and fidgeted with her phone.

"The time is here," Ray said to her. "They'll come out in a few minutes. You look good. You look like a lawyer."

"You think I was going to dress like a stripper?" She smiled at him. "You dress for court."

"You're not alone, as I said. We have other witnesses."

"Okay."

They had three witnesses now: Price, Augustina, and Mrs. Farrell. One was good, two was better. Three witnesses was unreal, like going from a cheese plate in a buffet line to a seafood dinner at a five-star restaurant. They could pull up some chairs, elbows on the table, and wade into the evidence.

A court officer walked out of the courtroom and into the hallway. "Augustina Calderon!" he yelled. The court officer moved toward them. "Ms. Calderon, please step this way now."

Augustina got up, straightened her jacket, and walked into the courtroom toward the witness stand.

*   *   *

Ray and Tania watched the proceedings. By mid-afternoon of the second day, Augustina and the other witnesses had finished testifying. The evidence showing Langford was innocent was overwhelming. The judge had heard enough. He frowned, gathered himself, and looked out at the gallery. Then he turned toward the defense table and locked eyes with Langford.

"The evidence presented here shows a pervasive scheme of government misconduct that is deeply troubling, almost beyond belief. Harrowing criminal acts by police and gangsters, inseparable in their commission, led to the suppression of evidence in your murder trial over fifteen years ago."

"Here, evidence was presented that agents of the Commonwealth took part in a scheme to frame an innocent man for murder even while knowingly exposing other witnesses to criminal acts of violence, including rape, in order to buttress their case and protect their own. Here today, when heinous acts conducted by state law enforcement agents were revealed, the Commonwealth can only make an argument on why it should be allowed to keep the defendant in prison for a little while longer. Faced with allegations of submitting false testimony from multiple witnesses in a criminal trial, the Commonwealth does not contest the essential facts of its own naked corruption, its own systemic failure to supervise its police officers and prevent the kind of misuse of informants that has badly damaged the trust citizens have in their justice system. Instead, the Commonwealth argues the defendant is a flight risk. The evidence presented to this court is only the first ray of light shone on what is likely to be a sinister, disturbing pattern of government malfeasance."

The judge paused to look around the courtroom and then back at Langford.

"Mr. Langford, my words of apology cannot make up for your lost years. No one can do that. This court lacks the power to wipe away such wrongness, but to you, sir, I do apologize in the limited capacity of a judge weighing the acts of other actors in our justice system. I see absolutely no reason for you to be held for any further period of time. There is no flight risk. The world is a better place for what you, your investigator, your lawyer, and the entire legal team did in this case. The example of your supreme character in surviving this ordeal is a beacon to us all.

"Further hearings will be held on this matter but for now, Mr. Langford, you are free to go."

The courtroom erupted in gasps and cheers. Langford put his face in his hands.

Tania turned to Ray and embraced him. He felt an overwhelming sense of gratitude. The long-awaited moment had come to pass. Sam Langford was walking out of the courtroom a free man. This was a victory they would never forget, something that surpassed all the brutal losses and delayed justice on other cases. A torrent of pure joy flooded his whole being. There was noise around him, voices shouting, the courtroom vibrating with pent-up emotion.

Ray and Tania looked on as a gaggle of lawyers smiled at Langford from the back row, some of them with such smooth, youthful faces that they looked like college students. He wasn't sure who they were, probably part of another legal team. The thought occurred to him that not so many moons ago, Sam Langford looked like those students. He was no longer young. But he was free.

Langford walked with Stone toward the exit as if harboring an unsteady feeling in his legs. Langford met Ray's glance in the back of the courtroom and gave him the thumbs up sign. Langford moved toward him and grabbed him hard around the shoulders.

"Thank you!" The men held each other.

"We did it," Ray whispered. Words did not suffice, and they just stood there, grinning at each other like children. Langford never accepted the word prison. In the end, even with his body held in captivity, Langford's imagination went beyond the body and over the wall.

Ray turned around and introduced Tania. Langford grabbed her hand, but other people were reaching for him, trying to get sprayed by some legal stardust. Ray noticed an older man with silver hair and an attractive younger woman who looked like kin—Langford introduced his father and sister. "Thank you for what you've done," his father said.

"My mother never lived to see this day. And I can't even cry," Langford said. He shook his head. "Sometimes I wonder, did prison make me hard? But it didn't make me cold. I love my family here," he said, gesturing to his father and sister. Then the entire group—the Langford family, Ray, Tania, and the defense team—surged like one joyous, multi-legged creature past the heavy wooden doors of the courthouse and moved towards the outdoors. They walked past the marble pillars out into the stone courtyard below the looming courthouse. The sunlight streamed down from the azure sky and they squinted in the sudden light. Ray noticed Langford striding taller than the last time he had walked away in chains.

The guards, the cops, the gangs, Langford outlasted them all. There was a spiritual thing to it, just taking it, more than anyone should have to, a ragged bone revelation. That was the awful secret, Ray realized. The discovery that you could endure anything.

THE END

ABOUT THE AUTHOR

John Nardizzi is writer and investigator. His crime novels won praise for crackling dialogue and pithy observations of detective work. He speaks and writes about investigations in numerous settings, including the World Association of Detectives, Lawyers Weekly, Pursuit Magazine and PI Magazine.

His work on innocence cases led to the exoneration Gary Cifizzari and James Watson, as well as million dollar settlements for clients Dennis Maher and the estate of Kenneth Waters, whose story was featured in the film Conviction. Prior to his PI career, he failed to hold any restaurant job for longer than a week. He lives near Boston, Massachusetts.

www.johnnardizzi.com
@AuthorPI

ALSO BY JOHN NARDIZZI

The Infantinto Files
TELEGRAPH HILL (Book 1)
THE BURDEN OF INNOCENCE (Book 2)
Book 3, forthcoming

Stay informed about future releases at
www.johnnardizzi.com or join the (very occasional)
newsletter by emailing johnf@johnnardizzi.com.

Honest reviews posted on any bookseller sites are
always appreciated. Thank you!

CPSIA information can be obtained
at www.ICGtesting.com
Printed in the USA
LVHW041450300322
714839LV00015B/697

9 781737 687603